THE ONE

WHO SEARCHED

LANCE LUCIANI

ISBN: 978-1-957351-48-3

The One Who Searched
Written by Lance Luciani
Edited by Megan Moyer
Cover Design: Lance Luciani
Cover & Interior Layout: Griffin Mill

Published by Nico 11 Publishing & Design
Mukwonago, Wisconsin
Michael Nicloy, Publisher
www.nico11publishing.com
mike@nico11publishing.com | 217.779.9677

Printed in The United States of America

This book is dedicated to the people in my life who have accepted who I am.

I am but a traveler only briefly stopping to admire the world.

THE ONE WHO SEARCHED

Prologue

October 2, 2013

The crisp fall air made for a perfect late morning as he contemplated his life's work. The sun was out, the humidity low, and the thermometer read sixty-six degrees. It was a good day to think about his life. He sat back and contemplated the information provided to him by his therapist. He thought about the events that had brought him to this place, his path.

He thought about how humans instinctually define success individually. There is a time limit on this life that seems to drive humans to leave a mark on the world, to in some small way define their life as complete. As Sean Rowe sang, "I'm just trying to leave something behind," which summed up his thoughts and reinforced his definition of success.

It would be that one path which, once set in motion, would achieve the outcome that the killer desired. This is what drove him. He stood on the top of the stairs of the Museum of Art in Philadelphia looking out over the city and viewing the George Washington Equestrian Statue in the not-so-far distance. Did the statue of the first leader of our country perched on his steed symbolize overcoming obstacles to create something? Or was it bigger than one person? For this one man, success would be defined by something else, a reckoning.

His mission was climbing each and every stair leading up to that perch, one at a time. His appetite grew with every step on the staircase. The thought of the kill: tearing lives apart like a predator ripping the meat off the bones of his prey. Slow and painful; satisfying and satiating to that appetite, leaving him to bask in the afterglow of a successful hunt.

It would right a wrong from something that happened long ago. Then peace would finally come to this killer.

Newton's first law of motion is: "An object in motion tends to remain in motion unless acted upon by an unbalanced force." A life can be derailed from its path by an unbalanced force. Life can also deviate from its path due to Newton's second law of motion which states: "If a larger object acts on a smaller one it causes acceleration." In life, a predator acting on prey can cause the acceleration from birth to death.

The world is full of predators and prey. It has always been that way and always will be. Life is the survival of the fittest. The weak perish as the strong conquer, the lion to the gazelle, the wolf to the rabbit; the human to every lesser species. But what about human-to-human conflict? Could that battle be won by intellect alone or is force also needed? These superior predators, who are at the top of the evolutionary lottery, are each vying for supremacy over the other in this winner-take-all, life-and-death game.

In that fight to the death, what determines who overcomes? Intellect or strength? Is the nature of the predator a predisposition, or is it created through experience? In animals, it is instinct based on thousands of years of evolution with one goal: survival. In humans, is it possible that the nature-nurture fight good and evil psyche can be swayed by certain events that occur in that individual's life? Or is it simply a fact that there are some humans who are naturally born with mental hardwiring which predefines them to hunt? The killer wants to know who he is. Therefore, he searches for answers to obtain an understanding of how he became the way he is. Is he a product of nature or nurture? Where does his story start and where will it end? Does anyone really know when death will come whispering, "It's your time"? Will it be death by a natural cause or will it be that predator that speeds death along its way? These are the questions to be answered. He hopes the answers will soon be revealed to him.

The killer thought to himself about hiding in plain sight. He thought about a song that described him perfectly. It was sung by Billy Joel, who sang about the faces of a stranger inside each of us and how we only allow ourselves to show them when alone.

CHAPTER ONE

BEGINNING OR ENDING

October 12, 2013
Monessen, Pennsylvania

It was a perfect Saturday morning. She was sitting peacefully under a tree in the middle of a place that the kids used to refer to as the "Tot Lot." She sat resting her head on her knees, facing a small pond where many kids and youths had caught their first tadpoles to keep as pets. They used small nets for capture and got the best results a couple days after a good rain. Rain brought the pond to life, full of noises and movement from the inhabitants. The kids soon found those tadpoles—which they called polliwogs—turned into smooth-skinned frogs, certainly not as cute as the tadpoles. After the novelty of the frogs wore off, and the kids realized the commitment of taking care of them was more than they bargained, for they would often return them to the pond to live out their lives in peace. Years later, the same kids, now in their late teens, drank alcohol and had their first awkward sexual encounters at that very same spot. These events were routinely taking place Saturday nights at the Tot Lot.

The Tot Lot contains a baseball field, home to the Bronco Baseball League of Monessen during the summer months. The league was comprised of boys 11 and 12 years old. The field was located just up the hill and through the trees from the pond. There were white oak trees that provided needed shade during the summer months and an amazingly beautiful display of reds and yellows before turning brown and falling to the ground to nourish the soil for the next year. There were also overgrown paths covered with slightly burnt grass due to lack of precipitation, which was typical of the fall season in this part of the country. The paths were barely visible to the naked eye after decades of non-use. Years ago, the paths were used by teenage boys riding high-powered motorbikes but those days were long gone. Those rides were a pure adrenaline rush of speed. That activity had given way to the new generation of adolescents who got their adrenaline rush from apps on their cell phones. Each one was vying for their "one minute of fame" by posting their current look and activities, no matter how trivial they were.

The weather was perfect for mid-fall in the Mon Valley area. The sun was out but it wasn't warm. The air was dry, and the smell of the change of the season comforting. The night before had been cold as it often was in this fall month, but now the golden streaks of the sun shone through the trees revealing something out of place in the white oaks and slightly burnt grass of the Tot Lot. Something that had not been there before. Something that, once found, would set in motion a chain of events and affect many lives.

At first glance, it appeared she was meditating from the way she was sitting, but appearances are not always as they seem.

CHAPTER TWO

THE TOT LOT

The dog ran ahead on the trail as he always did, his owner had no need to worry about him running off. The dog sniffed and explored without a care in the world, following the route that he and his owner traveled every day. Occasionally they crossed paths with a rabbit or squirrel, but today was different.

Domi stopped when he saw it, the thing that was out of place. Domi possessed a keen sense for things that weren't the same. Habit was his security in this world. And this woman, sitting under the tree, resting—or that's how it appeared—was out of place. He paused and then let his owner know of her presence. He barked loudly and aggressively, pouncing like a wild stallion. His owner ambled along the path to see what his dog was reacting to. Probably another rabbit or squirrel, he thought to himself. But this was not a rabbit or squirrel, it was a woman. When he saw how she was sitting, he first thought she probably had too much to drink the night before and was sleeping it off. He wanted to check to make sure she was okay so he said softly, "Miss," but there was no response. He said it a little louder and more commanding, "MISS," but still no response. He slowly moved close and touched her shoulder saying, "Are you okay, miss?" When she still didn't respond, he knelt beside her and gently lifted her head up with his hands, and then he saw why there had been no response.

After he realized what he was seeing, he jumped back two steps and froze, processing the image, his heart racing. This image would be burned in his mind forever. The girl had a single gunshot wound in the middle of her forehead. Her eyes were closed as if she were just resting. She had no pained expression on her face, no messy exit wound, simply a small hole slightly bigger than the size of a dime.

The man, Joe Kezner, called 911 immediately after regaining his composure. He was in his late fifties, with a full head of gray hair, and a slightly expanded mid-section that he vowed he was going to get rid of. He wore faded jeans, a plaid shirt, a light jacket, and hiking boots. His baseball cap sporting the Pittsburgh Steelers team logo in the traditional black and gold colors completed his southwestern Pennsylvania look. He had lived here most of his life, seeing the ups and downs of the Mon Valley. He was married to Jodi, his lifetime partner in crime. Their lives were normal and routine until this morning.

Joe removed his phone from his pocket, dialing 911 as fast as his shaking hands could move. "Monessen 911, what's your emergency?" said the operator in a calm, matter-of-fact tone.

He put one hand on his head and with the other held the phone to his ear. "I need help. I found a young woman. I believe she is dead," he said in a shaky, obviously distressed voice.

The operator was used to calls about accidents, break-ins, and, yes, even murders. It took a lot to shake her up or even surprise her anymore. "Sir, are you sure she is deceased? Have you checked for a pulse or heartbeat?"

Pacing in a small circle, he continued, "Ma'am, I'm sure she is dead because I can see a hole in her forehead. Can you send someone here quickly to help?"

"Absolutely. Please provide a location and I'll send a unit out right now."

Joe provided his approximate location and the operator was able to direct the closest Monessen Police Department unit there within 10 minutes of the call ending. Two cars arrived. The four officers wore the black uniforms synonymous with law enforcement, each sporting a silver badge with their number and name evident. Their side arms were holstered to their hips, along with other normal items. They were efficient at this routine because of their experience. They had mastered it after handling numerous murders, although none were similar to this one. Nonetheless, each knew their role well and started to work the crime scene efficiently.

The first two officers attended to the victim by quickly assessing her body. They first checked for a pulse and then a heartbeat. The lack of either confirmed that she was deceased. The other two officers started securing the crime scene. They followed crime scene protocol by taking Mr. Kezner aside for questioning. They tried to create a distance from her body so as not to disturb any more trace evidence that might get contaminated with activity. Mr. Kezner moved with the officers about twenty feet away from the scene, his dog was pacing nervously, as the Officers started gathering information about how he had come across the scene this morning.

Kezner told them he was very familiar with the area, and he and his dog, Domi, had traveled this same path daily around the same time for the past twelve years. Domi was a collie, yellow labrador mix, who always needed plenty of exercise. At twelve, he was starting to slow down, entering the twilight years of his life, but he lived for that daily walk. Kezner lived on Pennsylvania Boulevard in the third house up from the bottom of the street, located on the west side. From their location at the crime scene to his house would be seventeen to twenty minutes, depending on how many small animals Domi encountered, or smells he had had to identify. The daily walk provided Domi everything he needed: exercise, fresh air, and time with his dad. For Kezner, the walk allowed him to re-live his youth when he frequented the Tot Lot for various activities such as baseball, basketball, riding motorbikes, and later on, parties with alcohol and girls. Those were good memories and he savored them daily. They brought a sense of safety to him, like holding your mother's hand and feeling like nothing could harm you.

Joe worked for the Japanese-based company Sony. The Sony plant was located in the city of New Stanton, about eighteen minutes away by car. He had worked for Sony the past thirty years. Joe was one of the lucky ones who had acquired the job when the corporation built the plant in the late eighties to produce plasma screen TVs. Thankfully, the company provided a much needed boost to the local economy after the steel mills, US Steel and Bethlehem Steel, closed in the late seventies, relocating to Mexico which offered tax incentives and lower labor costs, a no-brainer for the steel giants to improve their bottom line.

Being a steadfast source of income, Sony sustained the small economies of nearby towns for decades. The once-pollution-creating steel mills, spewing their toxic smoke into the air, were now just rusting metal ghosts of companies, sitting along the Monongahela River with no purpose except to remind the former employees of better financial times.

Joe and his wife Jodi were glad they could stay in the area due to the low cost of living that southwestern Pennsylvania provided, and in another ten years he could retire comfortably with a pension.

But right now he was quite shaken to report the tragedy of a young woman whose life was taken away.

CHAPTER THREE

DETECTIVE BILL DROZD

Detective Bill Drozd, as usual, awoke early, ate, exercised, and showered before most people had even stirred. He received a call at 8:23 in the morning from the office, dispatching him to the scene of a crime—to be more accurate, a homicide. A female victim had been discovered by a man walking his dog in the early morning. His first thought upon receiving the call was about the integrity of the scene due to its location. If the weather had been rainy or snowy, the crime scene would be a mess, but instead, it had been crisp and dry overnight. This time of year the weather was a little bit more predictable. Drozd felt the weather was both a part of the charm and challenge of living in this part of the country.

It was early October, and seasons were changing. Soon the town would face the bitter winter months. Winters in southwestern Pennsylvania were easiest to understand by following this rule of thumb: the sun disappears in early November and doesn't reappear until late April. Grey is the color of the sky for those five months—a depressing period for most residents.

Drozd had just turned forty. He was of Ukrainian dissent, sporting blondish-brown hair and blue eyes. His face was clean shaven and had been since he was a teen.

He kept his hair cut tight to his head, not quite a military cut. He didn't look his age and was often mistaken for being much younger. He was 5'11" and in pretty good shape, tipping the scales around 175 pounds. He knew he was nearing middle age so he worked hard to maintain his health. He ran regularly and kept up with his weight training regimen which had made a difference. He was considered a catch.

He didn't like to wear suits to work like some detectives, but instead preferred a pair of jeans with a white button-up shirt. He looked like a guy who was comfortable in his own skin, comfortable with a relaxed style of dress.

He had never married. He had been close a few times, but then the inevitable happened each time, his job got in the way. He was driven by his desire to do a little bit better, to dig a little bit deeper, to find what others missed, and to put away bad people. This was his definition of success, and the women he had dated didn't want to play second fiddle to his job, and he couldn't blame them. After much soul searching, he knew the job would hold him back from a "normal" life consisting of relationships and eventually maybe even a family. His other vice, savoring many cups of coffee daily, made him rely on the caffeine way too much. On the positive side, he had read a report that coffee was good for you, and he decided to just take that as a solid truth, as a win in his life.

He had moved back to Monessen eight years ago from Ohio where he had started his law enforcement career after college. He had wanted to live in the northern part of the country, someplace consistent with his rural upbringing, but large enough so he could further his career. He had taken the position as investigator in Monessen after spending four years as an officer in the Columbus, Ohio, area. The job there had offered great experience with a mixture of major and minor crimes, but wasn't quite the war zone he faced when he moved back to Monessen to become a detective. He was happy to return home to the town he had grown up in. In Columbus there was no room for advancement as many of the officers were lifelong servants, and that contributed to his choice to move back. In Monessen, he would be the one and only detective.

Here he had been effective solving gang-related drug crimes but he knew it didn't really require extraordinary intelligence. Usually it was a drug deal gone bad, a gang member disrespected, or another factor that set an individual off. He was content in Monessen because he was responsible for his own success or failure. There wasn't a large bureaucracy to navigate so he could get shit done.

Drozd had arrived on the scene forty minutes after the call and the scene had already been taped off to ensure all potential evidence remained in place. They had to call the state police to send a forensics team since Monessen was much too small to fund a division of its own. The closest unit was in Belle Vernon, located just to the south. It took them 30-40 minutes to get there so they arrived just ahead of him by a few minutes.

Detective Drozd worked his way down the hill toward the crime scene. He walked slowly, taking note of the steepness of the path which leveled out in front of the small pond. "Hey, Nicky," Drozd said, as he came up behind Officer Melacrinos, slightly startling him. He stopped about twenty feet away and covered his shoes.

Officer Melacrinos shrugged it off and said, "Hey, Bill," as he continued to guard the scene while the forensics team did its job.

Drozd asked, "Had anything been touched before you got here?"

Melacrinos was shifting his weight from his left foot to his right foot and gestured to Drozd with his hand. "Nothing except for the person who called in the scene. That would be Mr. Kezner over there. Kezner got a close look at her but the ground was cold last night and I personally couldn't see any tracks, not even Mr. Kezner's."

Drozd had his pen and notepad out, and after getting the okay from Melacrinos, he moved closer so he could crouch down to examine the ground around the body.

Nicky Melacrinos was one of the four on-duty officers that had arrived on the scene first. He was 6'3". He sported jet black hair and was very muscular. He was of Greek dissent and an intimidating figure which was effective in Monessen with its special flavor of crime.

Detective Drozd was scanning for anything that the other officers might have missed. Looking up he asked, "Nobody else reported shots or saw anything suspicious?" He stood from his crouched position and swiveled his head side to side trying to see if any houses were within sight but all that he could see were trees and hilly terrain. The closest location with inhabitants was a dead-end road which was situated at the entrance to the parking lot of the Tot Lot and that was a good distance away.

Officer Melacrinos, hands on hips, furrowed his brow, removed his cap and ran his fingers through his hair saying, "This place is just a little too secluded for noise to carry but not secluded enough to hide something permanently. We're starting to canvas the area, but it's about a mile to the nearest houses so I wouldn't hold my breath that there were any witnesses."

Drozd had never seen such a neat and tidy crime scene in all his years on the Monessen Police Force. He had seen his share of murder scenes, but this differed from the norm—those that were tied to the city's new main industry: drug trafficking and distribution. The town had thrived in the seventies thanks to the steel plants that lined the Monongahela River, but those were long gone. The plants moved out and crime moved in, a simple supply and demand economics model.

Drozd was puzzled because the usual crime scene in Monessen was bloody carnage from automatic gunfire sprayed from passing cars. Often victims would be missing large parts of their anatomy. This insanity was due to the large number of semi-automatic weapons in this area which were capable of inflicting great damage to any unfortunate object or soul that got in their path. Gangs pointed their weapons with less than sniper-like accuracy, then aimlessly fired until someone was hit and that was almost guaranteed death. But this shooting was different, this was professional. It almost looked like a mafia hit, but a young woman victim was unheard of because usually families were off limits unless there were extenuating circumstances.

There were some old-school Italians residing in Monessen, but he didn't think of them as the organized-crime types. Many were masons, painters, and other skilled trade workers who were just following the tradition of their culture in regards to their choice of profession. But the fact was it was an execution-style hit and a tidy crime scene. At this point, he guessed anything was possible until the facts started to rule out options.

As Drozd jotted down a few notes, he noticed the way the body had been posed. It threw him off because she looked so peaceful and relaxed. She was simply sitting with her knees slightly bent, her arms resting on her knees, and her head resting on them. It was as if she were just putting her head down for a quick nap or to ponder life for a moment. Another puzzling thing was why someone would want her to be found. Most homicide victims were buried in at least a shallow grave to conceal the crime. Last, and most perplexing, was why time was taken to clean the victim so thoroughly. He guessed it might have been to remove trace evidence. But that would take time and energy. The killer would have to pay attention to detail and be very methodical. Was the killer OCD? Was that something that could help him in his investigation? Normal homicides were messy and random. The killer would be more concerned with concealing and fleeing the scene. Was staging the body a sign of a serial killer? His intuition was telling him something was different. Then he came back to his senses and thought, maybe I'm just reading way too much into this.

He went back to work, meticulously reviewing the crime scene, and concluded it was his job as an investigator to analyze everything from different points of view.

CHAPTER FOUR

Processing the Scene

Crime-scene technician Jeff Forlini took pictures of the entire scene using the grid method that the state police department adhered to as protocol. They called it square processing. After cordoning off the area he covered his shoes with disposable covers. He moved methodically from square to square, photographing each particular area with wide shots and then close-ups, hoping to catch anything that might be significant. This crime scene revealed a lot of nothing from his point of view. The coroner, Candice Collins, was carefully bagging the hands of the victim to preserve any trace evidence that might be under the fingernails. They had done this many times in Monessen but usually there was a lot more evidence strewn over large crime scenes.

"Hi, Candice, how have you been?" Drozd asked in an upbeat tone. They had worked numerous cases together and had even gone to dinner once or twice. She was an attractive brunette with large brown doe eyes. She wore black rimmed eyeglasses which completed her studious persona. She had a slight figure with curves in all the right places.

She replied back, "By now you know I'm ALWAYS good. You haven't called lately," she said in a jesting, playful manner.

Flirting back, he said, "Well, you know, I've been solving crimes and saving the innocent, which has kept me pretty busy." They both laughed and then returned to their respective tasks. "Do we have any ID on the victim?" asked Drozd, speaking in a more professional manner.

Candice continued wrapping the last rubber band around the wrist of the woman, securing the plastic bag. She looked up at Drozd, squinting a bit from the sunlight, and, shaking her head slightly, she said, "She's a Jane Doe for the moment until we can run some prints. She didn't have an ID on her but we did recover a phone from her back pocket. The bad news is its passcode locked so no immediate help there right now."

Drozd stood above Candice shifting his weight from one foot to the other and remembering the very nice evening they had spent together about three months ago. He asked, "Any idea on time of death?"

She could tell by the look on his face that he was thinking about more than the case, and, feeling good about herself, she almost smiled. Containing herself though, she said, "Well, it's been less than twenty-four hours, but the cold temps last night probably slowed the body temperature cooling process down slightly, so for now, let's keep it a bit broad and estimate time of death between 10:00 p.m. and 2:00 a.m."

She added, adjusting her glasses, "The person who discovered the body," checking her notes, "a Mr. Joe Kezner, says he walks this path at the same time every day, so she wasn't here twenty-four hours ago." Mr. Kezner lives not far from here, and he's available to speak with you. I have his contact information." She stood up using her gloved hands to wipe some dirt from her knees. She continued, "We will narrow it down more once we can get her identification and initial processing at the lab."

Drozd's mind returned to his first observation of the body and asked, "Any idea why there isn't much blood from the wound?"

She scrunched her cheeks upward, like she was biting a sour lemon, and stated, "Obviously a small-caliber weapon at close range but, it's strange because I would expect more blood, also, but there's none. It's almost like the wound was cleaned."

Now it was Drozd's turn to squint from one eye and clinch his forehead. "Cleaned? Never heard of a tidy killer in a Monessen scene as far as I can remember" sounding quite skeptical.

Candice shrugged, "Guess we'll figure it all out soon. I just need to get her back to the lab and do a full work up."

The wind blew lightly, and the sun was high by 10:30. Drozd knew this would be a long day. The coroner's vehicle had parked at the top of the parking lot which was about a half-mile away from the scene. As soon as they finished processing the scene for evidence they would transport Jane Doe to the morgue to start determining the exact time and cause of death.

Over two hours later they were ready to move the body to the ambulance for transportation. The EMTs gently lifted Jane Doe into a body bag and zipped it up. They lifted the bag onto the gurney and wheeled it up the steep path as gently as they could. About fifteen minutes later they lifted her into the ambulance. By now there were people in the parking lot, gawking to get a view. Something like this just didn't happen that often in this part of town.

There was no need for sirens or flashing lights. They pulled out and headed for the hospital in Charleroi, a small city across the river. Upon arrival, they removed the gurney and took it to the morgue where the pathologist would determine the cause of death.

28

CHAPTER 5

OUR FATHER

The screen displayed the text reply from psychiatrist Charlotte Burnett.

Charlotte was 5'8" with long brown hair and dark black eyes. She had a great smile, and people often told her she resembled Demi Moore. But she was more than just a pretty face. Burnett had graduated in the top twenty of the class of 2003 at the University of Michigan with an advanced degree in psychology. She was 38 and still single, although she had been close to marrying once while attending Michigan, but it hadn't worked out. They both wanted to pursue careers and neither of them would sacrifice that. Upon graduation her job offers had been on the east coast and his life was on the west coast. They both agreed long distance relationships never worked out so they had gone their separate ways. Now she was trying to pay off massive school debt and was forced to take this job for an online therapy application which provided the necessary flexibility so she could work another full-time job and keep up with loan payments and her current living expenses.

During the day she worked as an entry-level high school advisor for the mental health development department of Berry High School. She thought it was going to be a rewarding job, working with kids and gaining experience. But to her chagrin, her job was mostly filling out paperwork and occasionally setting protocol for how mental health situations were handled within the school system. It certainly wasn't what she expected, and to add insult to injury, the job paid a whopping $42,000 a year. Ten years of school to live in poverty.

She promised herself that this was temporary and that she would soon be able to start her own psychiatric practice. She looked forward to looking into the eyes of the people she was assisting instead of staring at a screen. Counseling patients via a computer was not ideal because facial expressions gave signals that words on a page couldn't provide.

Slamming the bottom portion of her fist onto her desk, she said to herself, "No fucking way to do this correctly," then hit *send* on her iPad. Off went the email and another $37 would get deposited into her bank account within two weeks.

The response to her client, Daniel Holiday, was protocol from the company in regard to how the therapy was supposed to be administered.

She was supposed to dissect their information and lead them down a rudimentary path to discover the foundation of their problems. Rudimentary was an understatement. The guidelines from the owners of the website were simple: "Don't upset them, because if you do, they won't pay." She blindly counted on the patient to be honest with her. Then she would gain an understanding of what that particular client deemed success. This would determine the detail that she would provide. She assumed this type of client wasn't likely to be suicidal. She felt at least this level of treatment didn't qualify for malpractice. Most of the time the client simply wanted to bitch about how bad their lives were. She would then console them and give a couple of "helpful suggestions" to push them in the direction the protocol dictated. She knew the main goal was to keep them paying for the service. She longed for a deeper challenge, but for now, she needed to pay her bills.

This specific client seemed to just say what she led him to say. He never really revealed much except for the normal parental, women, and pent-up anger issues. But that was the norm, or so she thought.

Dan Holiday wrote:

My father made me work doing chores for my allowance. One day his list included washing the car. It was a very large car, and it took me forever to finish It was a brown Pontiac Safari station wagon which could seat nine people and was probably one of the least attractive cars ever built. The good news was it was so large that I could fit the entire team in the car to drive to lunch when the cafeteria at the school served inedible selections. This chore was very time consuming. I had to wash it on a Saturday instead of being out with friends because, according to my father, that was the best day to get things done. After complaining for a short time, I shut up and washed the car. My back hurt and I was soaked, not to mention I had shut my finger in the door which was very painful and caused nasty bruising. When I was finished, my dad wanted to inspect my work. He walked slowly around the car and found one spot I had missed. He pointed at the area underneath the passenger side middle panel. I rushed to grab my wet rag claiming, "No problem, I'll just wipe that down right now, dad." But he wasn't going to hear of that. His code was broken. In a matter-of-fact tone, pointing at the spot, he said, "Do it right the first time."

"Now start over and do it again." That was another hour of work, at least. I had practice to get to. But to him that didn't matter. I had to stay and do it over again from scratch. Why was he like that?

Her response back read:

Dan, he was probably trying to teach you the importance of doing a job correctly. Was he tough on you? Of course he was, but did you learn from that experience? I'm sure you are very efficient and methodical—capable of completing a task by taking your time to make sure it is done right the first time. Do you resent your father for that? I know that you don't have your own kids, but can you understand his intention? I believe he did what he thought best to make his point.

What was your father's job? Do you remember anything about his relationship with his mother?

Later that day Dan opened the application and read her response. As he sat back in his chair, he said to himself, "My grandmother dominated my dad."

He waited the appropriate three days to respond to all her questions. It cost $260 per month for this online therapist who would respond twice a week per the terms and agreement. Absurd, he thought.

CHAPTER SIX

HELLO SHELLY LYNN

Detective Drozd picked up the phone. He could see it was the coroner, Candice Collins.

He put the handset to his ear and said, "Detective Drozd here, can I help you?"

"Bill, Candice here," she replied. "We have ID'ed your gunshot victim from the Monessen homicide through dental records. Her name is Shelly Lynn, age twenty-seven, from Bentleyville. DMV has the address as 463 Washington Drive." He was scribbling down notes as quickly as she could speak in his pretty indecipherable handwriting. He would translate them later as he always did.

Bentleyville is a borough in Washington County in southwest Pennsylvania, founded in the 1950s. It is twenty miles southwest of Monessen, west on Interstate seventy. The entire town is 3.7 square miles, all land, and its population is approximately 2,600.

Drozd wondered why she was found all the way in Monessen.

She was a long way from home.

Snapping back to the present, he asked Candice, "Is there anything besides the bullet in the head from your initial findings?"

She was all business today, no flirting, no small talk. He wondered if she was mad because he hadn't called socially since their last date.

She stated, "A small .22 caliber bullet, not from a normal .22, but most likely a .22 magnum. There was no exit wound, so the bullet was still in there. I'm still waiting for toxicology reports to come back. Time of death was between eleven o'clock in the evening and one in the morning. Like I said before, the cold probably slowed down the rigor mortis process."

Candice changed tones to a more emphatic voice, "I can tell you she was killed somewhere else and moved, and it had to have been done quickly. The blood pooled while she was in the sitting position. She might have been placed in a sitting position once she was relocated. If the trip were long, the blood would have pooled or rested on a side of the body or on her back—however she was positioned. It would have been evident in our examination. This also would account for why there is little evidence at the crime scene because it wasn't where the crime was committed," she stated.

Bill said, "Huh? Now I'm really confused. It's as though he wanted someone to find her there," airing his thoughts.

His next train of thought shifted to determining if rape was the motive. "Were there any signs of rape or trauma?" he asked.

Candice paused a second as if reviewing exactly what was written in her notes. "We examined her for rape. She definitely had recent intercourse, but there was no bruising or trauma, so I'm going to have to say it was consensual intercourse. Unfortunately, whoever she had sex with wore a condom and left no traces of semen or any other source of DNA."

Changing the topic to the characteristics of the bullet, she stated, "Ballistics is still inspecting the bullet for specific gun signatures to determine if that gun might have been used in another crime. If it was, we could get a lead on who it is registered to."

Bill had a grasp of the big picture based on the information Candice had provided. He knew he had a lot of work to do. He had to determine motive, means, and opportunity. So far he just had the name of the victim. He would have to start there. Ending the call he said, "Okay, Candice, keep me posted on what else you learn."

Finally letting her guard down, she quipped, "For you, almost anything"—their inside joke. The joke was that because they weren't exclusively in a relationship there were some things not included in what they would do for each other.

He chuckled, said, "Goodbye," and hung up.

Drozd sat back and thought about Shelly Lynn for a moment, her brownish blonde hair and thin build, similar to a runner or someone athletic. He'd have to find her next of kin, which he dreaded. This was one of the worst parts of his job.

He started by searching the Pennsylvania driver license database. He found a match quickly, including the next of kin in the emergency contact information. Shelly was also listed as an organ donor but that was no longer relevant. The emergency contact, her mother, was Terri Lynn, who had the same address listed on Shelly's license.

CHAPTER SEVEN

SHOCK AND AWE

Detective Drozd drove up to the Lynn house. It was a small, ranch-style home, which was very popular in the seventies. Tan, and set back from the road with a white fence around it, there was a driveway leading up to the white garage door, like most homes in Bentleyville. The population was small due to the lack of industry. There were few means of making a livable income in Bentleyville, and not much else that made it an appealing place to live. It did have a low cost of living and most residents liked the small-town atmosphere. This is what Terri Lynn liked.

Drozd walked up to the door and knocked. There was no doorbell, so he had to knock loudly. He did not want to call out as this was going to be a very emotional discussion and didn't need to start any sooner. It took what seemed like five minutes, but in reality, was less than sixty seconds, for Terri Lynn to open the door. Drozd noted she was approximately 5'7" and around 125 pounds, with light brown hair and brown eyes. He estimated she was in her late 40s or early 50s. She was attractive in a "girl-next -door" kind of way. She wore jeans and a button-down, plaid blue shirt and was understatedly attractive.

"How can I help you?" she asked with a puzzled look on her face. Terri tilted her head slightly to one side and brought her hand up to her chin, her other arm now resting underneath her elbow. She had no clue that her world was about to be turned upside down.

Drozd had his hands behind his back in a professional posture. He tried to keep his voice slow and steady. "Ms. Lynn?"

"Yes. Who are you?" she responded back quickly.

Drozd responded, even toned, "I'm Detective Drozd from the Monessen Police Department," as he reached in his back pocket and took out his identification. "Can we speak inside for a moment please?"

"What is this in regard to?" she asked, starting to shift her weight from one foot to the other keeping her eyes locked with his.

"Maybe we should discuss this inside Ms. Lynn," Drozd said, still even toned. He was sympathetic to the loved ones that he had to deliver bad news to and tried to put himself in their shoes. He tried to always be professional and respectful.

They went inside the house, which was modestly furnished with a homey feeling. The living room set consisted of a sofa, loveseat, and chair, most likely purchased at Rooms to Go on the extra-long no-interest payment plan. The furniture was mint green complemented by light wood, with well-worn end tables and accessories that matched. Obviously, Terri preferred the shabby-chic decorating style, evidenced by the light-colored tones and worn look of the furniture. The curtains were open to keep the room cheery and light-filled during the day. As he scanned the room Drozd noticed a picture of Shelly and Terri together at a park with a waterfall in the background. He thought it looked familiar, most likely the state park in

Ohiopyle, Pennsylvania, in the Laurel Mountains. It was famous for its waterfalls, fishing, and whitewater rafting. The smiles on their faces depicted a time that would stand still forever. Their strong mother-daughter bond was evident.

"Please sit." Drozd directed her to take a seat on the loveseat as it was closest to her. At first she declined, but after some insistence she lowered herself into the loveseat. If she fainted, he didn't want her to fall and injure herself.

Drozd spoke slowly and steadily as he started to tell Terri the awful news. "Ms. Lynn, this is in regard to your daughter, Shelly. Shelly was found this morning," he said, stammering to get the words out.

"Found? She was lost? She's okay, right?" she said in rapid succession. "Can I see her?" The blood was draining from her face, and Drozd worried she was going to faint. He was glad she was sitting down.

Drozd lowered his eyes and dropped his head slightly. His hands folded onto each other, almost as if in prayer.

She started to shake immediately and managed to say, "Not Shelly." She begged, starting to sob, "Not my Shelly!" She cried out, no longer trying to keep her composure.

Then it hit her, what he actually had conveyed. She was hysterical, and he could tell she was one step from going into shock. She trembled, and sobs were coming uncontrollably now. He moved closer and tried to comfort her. Drozd asked if there was someone he could call to be with her, but she said she was alone. At a later time, she would confide in him that her mother had passed seven years prior, and there was no husband. She also told him Shelly's dad was a quick affair and that had only resulted in Shelly. She had never regretted the affair for one moment.

Shelly became her purpose in this world.

He held her for what seemed like an eternity, knowing it was that contact that was the only thing helping Terri hold on to her sanity. She tilted her head onto his shoulder and tears were streaming down her face and onto his shirt. He reached into his pocket for a handkerchief. He had learned that when delivering bad news which often resulted with emotional outpourings, it was imperative to have one ready. He handed it to her to wipe her tears away. After about twenty-five minutes she settled just a bit, but he knew that she was just accepting the news she had just received.

He started to tell her the general outline of the events of the previous day without specifics. She was still not doing very well. He asked if it would be better if he came back later but she shook her head through the tears. So, he continued on very gently and professionally. He told her about where Shelly was found and some particulars, eventually assuring her that there was no sexual motive involved. He purposefully left out some of the details that were a classified part of the investigation.

At the end, he finally called her neighbor with the phone number Terri provided him. The woman arrived not long after the call. She was a kind, older woman named Victoria Kirkpatrick. She and Terri had been there for each other on numerous occasions, supporting each other through tough times. When she showed up, she moved quickly through the door and past Drozd, arms extended, reaching for Terri. They embraced and Victoria started to become emotional. She was remembering Shelly taking her first awkward steps as a toddler and progressing to a full run months later. Victoria was "Aunt Vicky" to Shelly. Terri was in good hands, but Drozd knew that it was going to be a long night and that her life was just turned upside down now that her only child had been taken away.

With Victoria by her side holding her hand, Terri started to recall what she knew about Shelly's movements and whereabouts the night before. Terri knew that Shelly had gone out, assuming that she was staying with her boyfriend. His name was Gavin Dean. Gavin and Shelly attended a regional college in western Pennsylvania together in Belle Vernon, just fifteen minutes away. She had often stayed with him at his small apartment on Main Street in downtown Belle Vernon after classes. Terri had accepted that her daughter was old enough to make her own decisions and that had kept their relationship healthy.

Terri told Drozd his address and described the general location of Gavin Dean's apartment. She had only been there once to drop Shelly off. They gently spoke about her suspicions that the couple had been having some problems as of late, but she couldn't believe that he was capable of doing anything to Shelly, or at least she hoped.

After running through all the questions that he had on his list, his face turned somber. Drozd said softly, "Ms. Lynn, I'm going to have to ask you to come with me to the morgue to identify Shelly. You are her only family. I'm sorry to have to put you through this, but it is necessary. I know it's going to be extremely tough, but I'll be right there with you.

Terri was barely coherent at this point, but she nodded her head, she was still softly sobbing. She looked up and asked when she was needed and where Shelly was located.

Drozd said he would come back later that day and personally drive her. Then he would bring her home afterwards, make sure she was okay, and had everything she needed. Victoria held onto Terri's hand, gently caressing it, trying to soothe and comfort her friend. She hoped she could help Terri in some small way.

Terri shook her head up and down slightly. Her eyes filled with tears as she looked at a spot on the wall. It was like she was looking right through Drozd. It didn't even register with her when he stood up and started to make his way to the door. She made no movement to show him out.

Drozd said, "I'll be back around two this afternoon to take you there Ms. Lynn." There was no response, but he assumed she had heard him and would be ready. "Victoria if you want to come, I have no problem with that."

Terri said quickly, her eyes darting up, "No, I need to see my angel by myself," then returned her eyes to the floor.

Drozd made his way out the door on his own. He started making notes in his notebook while he walked to his car. He thought, here is a lead that might help solve the case quickly. It's probably just a crime of passion. This would be another example of life in Monessen, routine and predictable.

CHAPTER EIGHT

ANGEL

The drive was not far but time almost stood still in the car that transported Terri Lynn from her house to the morgue which was located at the Mon Valley Hospital. They drove down the interstate with only light traffic. Drozd kept to the speed limit and exited at the appropriate time from the highway. The exit sign read, "Charleroi and Speers." This exit was located right after the bridge that crossed over the Monogahela River which separated Belle Vernon from Charleroi. Drozd drove cautiously. He took the road, the river on the rider side, into the main town of Charleroi. Charleroi, Pennsylvania—named after the Belgian city— was a small borough right on the Monogahela River. Many Belgium immigrants resided here, arriving at the end of the 19th century. Some of them were glass makers so it was no surprise the town was the home of the Corning Glass Company. Later, Corning became Corelle Brands, which still produces glass products at a major factory in Charleroi, helping to sustain the economy of the Mon Valley. Drozd and Terri continued to drive, until they reached the hospital entrance. Drozd drove to the lower entrance. He assisted Terri, helping her out with a gentle hand to support her. He told her to wait in the entrance while he parked the car.

He was back in a couple of minutes as promised, but he knew that to Terri it probably felt like an eternity. They made their way to the elevators, and proceeded down to the next level. The doors opened to the reception area. The walls had pictures of tranquil forests and wildlife and was lit with white florescent bulbs which gave it a sterile, stark feel like a doctor's office. It smelled of the cleaning solutions used daily to keep the floors sterile. But in reality it was the morgue. With her arms crossed and her eyes down, Terri walked forward like a defeated person, not having said a word during the whole trip. Drozd could see the dread on her face, the lines in her forehead protruding, so he knew that she was close to losing her sanity.

Drozd escorted her to the desk, and the receptionist called the pathologist to let her know they were being sent back. Taking Terri's hands in his and looking her in the eyes, Drozd said, "Are you going to be okay, Ms. Lynn?" Terri shook her head, yes, with the slightest motion but didn't hold eye contact with him. In her state of mind, she probably wasn't sure of the true answer to his question.

Terri and Drozd walked to the double doors, and he hit the button to automatically open them. He had been here many times and was familiar with where to go. They stepped inside where they were united with the pathologist in charge of the autopsy, Doctor Margaret Bolet, a woman of slight build in her early 50s, was wearing a white lab coat with her name embroidered on the left side of her chest.

"Ms. Lynn," she said, "I'm Dr. Bolet," as she extended a hand for support.

Terri took her hand, Drozd right by her side. They paused for a moment so Terri could catch her breath and prepare for what would be the hardest and worst moment of her life.

He asked, "You okay?"

She nodded with a just a slight movement of her head. Drozd and Bolet had worked together before, so each knew what was ahead for Terri Lynn.

Dr. Bolet led them to the table where Shelly's body was draped with a white sheet. She had waited to remove the top of Shelly's skull until after the identification was made. She was able to extract the bullet without making large incisions.

She pulled back the sheet far enough for Terri to see Shelly's head and face. Here it was, the worst moment of Terri's life. She held her eyes closed for a moment and then opened them and gasped at the face of her baby girl. She wanted to believe this was just a bad dream and a terrible mistake. She didn't scream or cry uncontrollably, not yet. She had time to prepare for this inevitable moment over the last four hours. After what seemed to be minutes but in actuality was seconds, she simply nodded her head and started to sob slowly and softly. She asked if she could have a few moments alone with her angel and Drozd and Bolet graciously left the room.

Drozd leaned in quietly to Bolet and said, "Smart to keep her as much intact as you could until this was over." Bolet shrugged, stating somberly, "Doesn't make it any easier for her." She informed him that she hadn't found anything else helpful so far and didn't expect to. "There were no needle marks or anything that brought events leading up to or reasons for the murder itself any clearer," she stated. After a few minutes, she noticed Terri slightly gesturing to the two of them to return.

Bolet re-covered Shelly gently. Then she came back over to the detective and Ms. Lynn, motioning for them to follow her. Bolet escorted them toward the hallway, one hand on Terri's back and one hand on her arm for support.

When they reached the reception area Bolet said she needed one more thing before they left, a signature from Terri confirming that was Shelly's body. Terri looked up, her eyes filled with tears. She reached to start signing the form, but her hand was trembling, and she created unrecognizable slashes on the page. She gestured *goodbye* with a nod of her chin, slowly walking back toward the doors from which they had entered. She was a little unsure of her footing, but told herself, *one foot in front of the other.*

Drozd steadied her ,and upon getting her up to the reception area safely, he left through the front doors of the building, got the car, pulled around, and helped Terri back into the passenger seat. They followed the same route back to her house where he had called to make sure the neighbor, Victoria Kirpatrick, was able to be with her before he left.

Victoria was at the front door when they arrived and she helped Terri back into the house. Drozd watched them get in safely and backed down the driveway.

Driving back, he could only think about Terri. Her life gained purpose after having Shelly. Her purpose in life was creating another life. She had more than twenty-seven years of that responsibility and the joy that came with it. Now what would her new purpose be? Did she have enough things in her life to weather this storm and get past the tragedy that robbed her of her daughter? He wasn't sure if she would make it out of this dark time in her life, but he hoped she would.

Had he made a mistake in not starting a family to enjoy this purpose in life? He began to question everything.

CHAPTER NINE

THE NICE GUY

Detective Drozd drove his unmarked squad car toward the apartment of Shelly Lynn's boyfriend Gavin Dean. Dean's name and address had been supplied by Terri when he spoke with her right after her daughter's death. Today was the day Drozd would start questioning Dean. Drozd was hopeful for signs of his guilt, inconsistencies in his story, alibi, or even physical tells of untruths in his expressions or demeanor.

Dean was twenty-five, standing 6'2". He had dingy brownish-blonde hair and a scruffy beard which looked more like three days of a lazy growth. He was thin in build and had a slight curve to him due to bad posture. The one thing he had going for him was he was nice. The trait haunted him. Women said he was nice—not handsome, not mischievous, not dark and mysterious—just nice.

He worked a meaningless job at Home Depot stocking the shelves and answering endless questions from the do-it-yourself weekend warriors whose home projects were often doomed to fail but it was of no concern to him. The shoppers were from Belle Vernon and the surrounding area. It was Gavin's job to sell them items they needed and even some they would never use. He knew most would likely be too lazy to return them. The job paid decently, and more importantly, it allowed him to afford to attend entry-level college classes with the hopes of getting into a state school within the year.

He and Shelly had dated for four years. They met by chance when he saw her working at a local bakery. The Keystone Bakery was named after the familiar nickname for Pennsylvania, "The Keystone State." The bakery had been established and relocated numerous times through the years but always had the same amazing selection of breads and sweets. When you walked into the store your nose was rewarded with amazing scents! Since Gavin had a sweet tooth, indulging in treats from the bakery had become his bad habit of choice. One day he ambled into the bakery and WHAM, there she was! He felt as if a lightning bolt ran down his spine and he immediately became nervous as his pheromones went into overdrive. From that day, the combination of Shelly and the cakes and pastries sent his dopamine levels sky high. Especially one particular pastry, which resembled a crème hot dog in a pastry instead of a bun. They were made fresh daily and immediately addictive. Shelly worked behind the counter five days a week and his routine to try and get her attention included daily stops. Without his daily fix of the sweets and the beautiful girl, he felt he would crash. This routine made him feel alive, he didn't think about the potential long-term effects of his bad habit.

His perseverance had paid off after three weeks of daily stops. Shelly relented and agreed to go on a date with him. He had stammered through asking her out, trying desperately to sound cool. It didn't work, but she liked him because he was a nice guy. On their first date they couldn't afford anything fancy, so they settled on a trip to a popular fast-food restaurant, Bill's Golf Land, which served burgers, hot dogs, chicken, and other fast-food staples. It was a joint complex, connected to the golf driving range and miniature putt-putt course. Those amenities sat to the right of the restaurant. You could eat at the enclosed area looking out over the driving range and watch the action. They had a great time. The real bonus for Robert was seeing Shelly in her tight spandex shorts and crop top—he thoroughly enjoyed every single moment of that day. He would remember it as the best day of his life.

But something had altered the path of her life and accelerated her death. An outside force that subsequently changed the path of Gavin's life also.

CHAPTER TEN

DELAYED GRATIFICATION

Dan Holiday wrote:

The kids at school made me feel like nothing. I was poor and had to work many jobs as a youth to afford the extras so many of them were privileged to get without effort. All I wanted was to be like them and fit in. I considered them to be normal. I was very tired all the time because I had responsibilities that started early each morning until often late at night, causing me to fall asleep in class. I started work at 4:30 a.m. delivering newspapers, then went to school, and worked most nights stocking shelves and cleaning at a pharmacy to earn enough money to train for my chosen sport. Kids picked on me, calling me names that were hurtful. Sometimes the bullying became physical. I didn't and couldn't retaliate. I simply took it and pushed the pain down, down deep. I always kept my cool and pretended it didn't affect me. Inside it was different. Sometimes I was full of rage and destruction. It's a good thing I learned to be patient and can wait for success. I think delayed gratification is a skill not taught to youth of today, but I adhere to its painful process. There have been times I waited up to five years to succeed at something.

Therapist Charlotte Burnett's reply:

Dan, kids can be amazingly cruel. Some kids lash out and kill others for this reason, or they do harm to themselves. You demonstrated great resiliency getting through this difficult time of your life. You obviously did the right thing because you are now a successful member of your community. Did you tell your parents about these verbal attacks? If so, what was their advice?

He thought, *that was two more clues, Doc, but many more to come before the test.*

CHAPTER ELEVEN

Never Hurt Her

Detective Drozd parked on the street in front of Gavin Dean's apartment building. Unlike bigger cities, Belle Vernon had yet to implement street parking fees. The shops that lined the streets were not big chain businesses but more mom-and-pop, family-owned businesses, like Jake's Pizza, the small family-run corner market, and the locksmith, who had been there for many years, to name a few. He backed into a spot and turned the ignition off. Exiting the car, he walked to the door leading up to the apartment which was situated above a local retail shop. Drozd assumed that Dean's apartment would resemble the one he lived in during his college days at Michigan State University. He felt he was lucky to have been able to live the last three years of school in a small off-campus apartment while he studied and obtained his degree in criminal science.

He knocked on the door, and after a short pause, Gavin Dean opened it. His face was sunken, undoubtedly from lack of sleep and severe mental anguish. His bloodshot eyes were bleary and had a faraway look, similar to the one he had seen in Terri Lynn's eyes. He wore a black t-shirt with the logo of an outdated band.

"May I help you?" said Dean as he peered through the doorway.

Drozd replied with a very even tone. "Yes, Mr. Dean, I'm Detective Drozd from the Monessen Police Department," as he produced and showed his credentials. "May I speak with you for a few moments regarding Shelly Lynn?" he asked as he refolded his identification and put it into his back pocket.

The blood drained from Dean's face and it looked as if he was going to be sick as an obvious wave of nausea came on. He invited Drozd into his apartment with a gesture. Drozd looked around confirming his suspicions about the apartment. It was very similar to the one from his college days. The room was sparse of furniture but cluttered with things that should have been cleaned up and thrown away days ago. They stood a couple of feet inside the door, Drozd with a pad and pen in his hands. There was no offer of water or a beverage, but Drozd wanted to get down to business quickly anyway.

Dean looked up at Drozd getting his attention with intense eye contact. He started speaking quickly, "Shelly's mom called me last night screaming, 'What have you done? What have you done?' He was stammering. "She screamed that I had taken away her life by killing Shelly! Killing Shelly? What was she talking about? I could never do that. I didn't know why she was yelling at me, but she just kept screaming, 'Why? Why?' I told her it was impossible that Shelly was dead! Shelly can't be dead! It couldn't be true! But Terri just kept screaming and then slammed the phone down." Dean proceeded to tell Drozd, "Shelly and I met after class Thursday for coffee, but she left early because I had to go to work the next morning at six o'clock. Shelly is considerate like that," he stammered. "The last thing she said to me was that we would catch up after my shift on Saturday. I could never hurt Shelly, you have to believe that!" he blurted out, beginning to lose all composure. He put his fingers on his temples trying to stop the throbbing pain that was increasing in the right side of his head. The stress was getting to him.

Drozd was not sure what would happen next but pressed on, "So, you are saying that you were home alone Friday night between the hours of nine o'clock in the evening and two o'clock in the morning?" asked Drozd trying to establish the opportunity part of the trifecta of solving cases. Means, motive, and opportunity created convictions.

"Yes, I was here," he said softly. "I have to sleep so I can get up by 4:45 a.m. to be on time for work. We had coffee after class, which ended at 8:00 Thursday night. There's a Denny's down the road two miles from here where we met. The workers there can tell you we were there. We talked about the day and had our coffee. We had driven there in separate cars after class. She said she would head back to Bentleyville to her house, and I agreed without objection because I was tired. That night the class was tough, and I didn't have much time to study for the next day, so it made sense. I would never hurt Shelly...I loved her," he said in an almost pleading voice, hoping Drozd would believe him.

Drozd didn't see any obvious facial tells when Dean spoke but pressed on, trying to get him to change his story. Drozd scratched his head, saying, "You see from my point of view, this seems a bit convenient. I'm supposed to just believe that you were home alone after being the last one with her." He furrowed his brow, and said, "Her mom seems to think there was trouble between you and Shelly."

Gavin shot back aggressively, "That's bullshit!" even though his eyes shifted away. "We were close," he continued. "I was going to propose as soon as I got into the state university. I wanted to be with her and no one else."

There was a tell right there: "no one else." Why would he say that?

Was it a slip?

Recovering, Drozd went right back to his agenda as the voice inside him was saying, *come on kid make another slip*. He said, "Gavin, you see my issue with your timeline," continuing to apply pressure. Drozd was so glad that Dean was cooperating without a lawyer present. It made his job so much easier, why not give this guy the full court press?

Gavin lowered his head and muttered, "I would never hurt Shelly," his voice trailing off at the end.

Drozd wanted to give the guy a night to forget things he told him so inconsistencies could appear, so he chose to retreat for the moment. Drozd put his hands up in the air and said, "I think we will have to continue this conversation at the police station tomorrow, but until then, please don't leave the area."

Gavin Dean did not get up. He simply stared out the window blankly.

Drozd proceeded down the stairs and out the door onto the sidewalk. The road was not super busy but there were a few cars passing and a few people milling about. Upon entering his car, he placed a call to the district attorney to file for search warrants for Gavin Dean's apartment. He also placed a call to his superior to ask for a surveillance team to watch Dean's apartment overnight until he could interrogate him again tomorrow. He wanted to make sure that Dean wasn't going to conveniently leave, and his boss granted it without hesitation.

CHAPTER TWELVE

CONVENIENCE PLUS

Detective Drozd got signed warrants to search Gavin Dean's home executable the next day. He had assigned two officers to watch Dean's car, so they stayed on watch through the night trying to stay alert to any movement or exit. Those officers had specific instructions to follow and report in immediately if Dean made ANY movement from his apartment. Drozd felt confident he had a solid suspect and thought maybe his first assumption was wrong, the homicide hadn't been done by a professional. Maybe Dean was enraged and in an unstable state of mind when he shot Shelly Lynn in anger. Maybe after he realized what he had done, remorse had led him to clean the wound and take her to the place where he had placed her peacefully. It was a lot of *maybes*. Drozd hated *maybes*. He liked it when things lined up with confirmable events. That wasn't happening in this case so far.

Drozd returned to optimism as his mind raced quickly toward a quick conviction and the possibility of resting for the weekend with a beer and some mindless, senseless TV. He could be home on Sunday, able to watch the Pittsburgh Steelers with Ben Roethlisberger, Le'Veon Bell, and Antonio Brown playing in their crusade toward a Super Bowl run this year. Was this even possible? It had been quite a while since he had been able to thoroughly enjoy a day of nothing to do or worry about. Maybe he would even ask Candice Collins over to enjoy the game and maybe a bit more. She was good company, not to mention being very attractive. His thoughts drifted back to his earlier questions pertaining to relationships and children. It was starting to play on his mind.

Then he snapped back to reality and the job at hand. He wanted to compartmentalize his life right now, so he chased those thoughts away, but for how long? He ran through the sequence of proving a murder: means, motive, and opportunity. The search warrant would possibly give them the means, the motive was circumstantial, but the mother had given him the basis for that with the suspicion of infidelity, and the opportunity was there after they had coffee and Dean was alone in his apartment during the window of the time of death. Could it really be that easy? It felt just a little too convenient.

He had learned through his career that if you thought things to be simple that often led you to be complacent. When you are complacent, mistakes are often made. He had made mistakes before and always wanted to learn from them, not repeat them. With that in mind, he always took the extra time to think about things from different angles before trying to turn his assumptions into facts. He played chess when he got the opportunity and enjoyed what the game provided—the chance to think ahead and from different points of view. He felt Monessen hadn't challenged him yet. Crime here in Monessen seemed a bit easier, more straightforward than his time in Columbus law enforcement. Columbus had a variety of crime. In Monessen, crime was usually nothing special, just drugs and thugs. His talents were being wasted on these cases.

It left him unfulfilled, but his superiors had been happy with his ability to close cases. He felt he was very capable of much greater things.

CHAPTER THIRTEEN

RENDEZVOUS

When he was leaving Gavin Dean's apartment yesterday, Detective Drozd had told him they should meet at one o'clock in the afternoon at his office at the police station to review his story and alibi from the beginning. The overnight break might distract him enough to forget something or change something in the story. That's what Drozd was counting on. This would become a chess match.

Dean had still been in obvious distress and only nodded his head to agree to the time. He had looked at the ground as he sat and never made a move to see Drozd out. He was slouched over, shoulders drooping, his hands on his thighs, and his chin hung down. He hadn't showered and smelled of sweat. A man either full of loss, remorse, or guilt.

Drozd was running the questions in his mind, *Was he distressed because he got caught? Was he truly upset that Shelly was dead? What were the problems between them? Did he own a gun?* There were so many questions to be explored and Drozd was planning his chess moves to lead Dean down the path to confessing, thus ending the game.

When he started the questioning, he would present Dean with the search warrant for his car and his house. He didn't want to formally arrest him because he knew Dean would get a lawyer in the blink of an eye. Drozd wouldn't blame him. Later in the morning, the officers would be signaled as soon as the warrants were delivered and the searches could begin.

CHAPTER FOURTEEN

THE BEST OF THE BEST

Dan Holiday wrote:

I remember once when playing for the high school team I had just started to compete and the opposing team laughed at me because of my lack of ability. The summer after that incident I spent all my time practicing the skills they had made fun of. The time spent to master this was worth it and the next year I competed with those same kids at a new level. They didn't laugh after that. That satisfaction was well worth the work.

As a child I spent much time alone. I began to practice target shooting with a simple air compression gun. Then later I saved for and purchased a sport shooting pistol. My father had no problem with that purchase as long as I paid for it myself. He even helped with the paperwork needed to possess the gun. It was something that I enjoyed so thoroughly that I could do it ten hours a day. It became my obsession. My backyard was large enough that I didn't bother anyone, not my parents or the neighbors. I learned to shoot with one hand then the other until I would never miss the target. I would then add dimensions of challenge by moving and shooting, sprinting and then shooting so I had to learn to shoot with adrenaline flowing. I did this until I was perfect.

Everything I have done in my career and life have been about becoming the best at whatever I did. I strived for this no matter what it was. I would do whatever it took to be better than everyone. Why am I like this?

Therapist Charlotte Burnett's reply:

It sounds like it is your way of dealing with things that you find unacceptable. From the information you have provided me, I think you try and find ways to avoid confrontation. You push your anger deep down and have to find an outlet for it, so you try and be productive instead of destructive. It sounds like you have developed your own code of what is acceptable. The boys laughing at you drove you forward. The practice, and later success, was your way of dealing with them breaking that code.

When you were young, were you punished for speaking your mind? We have already established that you do have some self-confidence issues. We need to look further into why that trait is present in order to understand where this came from.

Can you tell me if one of your parents was abusive to the other? Was there a need for you to come between them?

Later, the killer thought, *Doc, are you trying to infer that I was a victim of co-dependency? That I had to buffer between my parents and therefore lost my childhood, so I grew up too fast? Very interesting observation. Guess I'm getting my money's worth.*

He sat back in his chair with his hands behind his head.

CHAPTER FIFTEEN

No Reply at All

Detective Drozd flipped his arm up and checked the time on his watch. It was 9:22 in the morning, and Drozd felt he had been patient, and decided it was time to act. It was still early enough that he thought Dean might not be sharp and completely coherent.

He had driven up quietly and parked a couple of cars down from the unmarked car of the officers assigned to keep surveillance on Dean's home. After he parked he used his microphone to tell the officers he was in position. He asked, "Has anyone left the apartment?"

Officer White replied that Dean hadn't left, and no one else had entered since their meeting the afternoon before. This information was also confirmed by the two officers who had been assigned to the late-night shift. They had worked until the early morning hours and then reported to Officer White when he took over in the morning. This was a good sign because Drozd had been concerned that Dean would flee the area. But the officers had been in place all night and they would have observed him if he had left because there was only one entrance to his apartment building.

With the report from the officer confirming no sightings, Drozd was ready. Officer White asked for further instructions.

"It's time to present Mr. Dean with the search warrants so let's approach carefully," said Drozd. "I want vests on for maximum protection."

The Kevlar vests provided a fair amount of protection for vital organs in case of gun fire.

Drozd said, "It's time to go knock on his door, but please use extreme caution. This guy is on the edge. Just tell him you have search warrants for his apartment."

He wanted the officers to present and conduct the initial search. He was also trying not to provoke Dean into calling a lawyer or invoking his Fifth Amendment right to remain silent until the conclusion of a second informal conversation with him. Playing the chess match, he stayed in the car—much to his chagrin—his heart was beginning to pump faster with adrenaline.

He was running the chess match in his mind, flipping the board back and forth. He was looking at the case from multiple perspectives. *I don't want to arrest him until I have a reason to. I'd prefer to try and talk to him before he finds a lawyer.* Drozd continued running scenarios. *If he gets counsel, it will lessen the chances of catching him by exposing inconsistencies in his story.* He knew that Dean was mentally on the edge yesterday, but he had no evidence yet to charge him with anything. He hoped the search of his house would give them something to work with, such as the gun, or in the trifecta of convictions, "the means."

The officer approached the door, knocked, and then announced, "Officer Terrance White with Monessen police, please answer the door."

Officer White had been a member of the Monessen police department for eight years. He was in his early thirties, tall and thin, standing 6' 3" tall and weighing 170 pounds. He was a light-skinned African American. He was so light skinned that he had often been mistaken for being of Latino or Italian descent, occasionally people just thought he had a nice tan. Officer White paused and announced himself again. He got no response.

Reaching up to the shoulder mounted microphone of his police radio, he asked Drozd for further directions.

With tension forming in his chest, Drozd's hands were moving nervously over each other. He quickly responded, "Well, you are in fear for the safety of the occupant, so force the entry."

Officer White replied, "Ten-four."

Drozd interjected, "Be careful this guy seemed…" but

Officer White cut him off, saying matter of factly, "Yes, we know you said before, USE CAUTION,"

Drozd responded, "Copy that."

Officer White signaled for his partner, Officer Sue Baker, to join him. She had been at the bottom of the stairs as back up, but now she was needed. She climbed the stairs to Dean's apartment and together they approached the door. Officer Baker was a plain Mon Valley Girl, with a solid frame of 130 pounds standing 5'2". She wasn't thin, but she wasn't a large person either. Muscular is how she described herself. She was a career officer, with the force for almost fifteen years.

She knocked on the door and announced herself, "Police Department."

She knocked again, but nothing. After getting no response, she tried the door, and to her surprise, it was unlocked.

She radioed back to Drozd about the door being unlocked and said, "We're going in."

She and Officer White slowly swung the door all the way open and left it that way. They entered into the small studio apartment, repeatedly announcing, "Monessen Police Department" numerous times.

They cleared the living room, moving in a staggered pattern. Their guns were drawn, and they were moving in unison quickly. There was only one room which doubled as the bedroom with a pull-out sofa bed. It was sparsely decorated, and they could quickly see there was no one there. No one was visible as their heads swiveled side to side scanning for any movement.

Finally, Officer Baker called out loudly to Officer White, "Clear."

They cautiously proceeded toward the bathroom, each with their issued side-arms drawn and at the ready ,expecting Dean to appear. They hoped he wasn't armed, but they had to take all the precautions possible.

The door to the bathroom was slightly ajar and the light was on but it was very quiet. Officer Baker pushed the door further open so they could enter. The small bathroom only had a sink, a toilet, and a bathtub. With a quick glance she saw it was decorated sparsely, with no pictures on the wall. The floor was white tile, cold, and unfriendly. Officers White and Baker slowly approached. Officer Baker entered with her sidearm ready, poised in front of her, her finger on the trigger. Her heart rate was high as the adrenaline pulsed through her body. *Use extreme caution*—the words running through her mind from the instruction given minutes ago by Detective Drozd.

Once in the bathroom the reason Gavin Dean was not answering their requests for entry was evident. He was in the bathtub. The water in the tub was crimson red. His wrists had been slit. His face was mostly out of the water. He was bluish in color. There was no life left in his body.

Both officers had seen death before, but it's not something one ever gets used to. It had such a sad cosmic finality to it, especially if it was caused by an outside force accelerating that person's path to the end.

Officer White pressed on the talk button of his shoulder-mounted mic, and asked the dispatch officer for an ambulance and the coroner. The word "coroner" was all Drozd needed to hear.

Detective Drozd said, *Fuck!* to himself, pounding on the steering wheel of his car.

The officers left the bathroom to look around the apartment, without disturbing anything. On a small grey desk which sat in the corner, they found a single white piece of paper by itself. On it was a handwritten note which simply read: *I don't want to live without you. You deserved better.* The words were barely decipherable. Whoever had written it obviously had been shaking badly.

They radioed to Drozd, delivering the news, but he had already heard the transmission for the ambulance and knew it was his worst nightmare.

CHAPTER SIXTEEN

REGRETS AND REALITY

Detective Drozd slammed his hand on the console of his car and cursed himself for not taking Gavin Dean into custody for twenty-four hours without charging him. He could have put him on suicide watch, taking away his opportunity to take the easy way out. It would have given Drozd another chance to speak with him, try to break his alibi, or at least create doubt by any discrepancies in his story. But looking at the other half of the chess board, he knew if he had, Dean would have lawyered up. It was a moot point now. Was it a mistake or just a move, like trading a bishop for a knight in a chess game, just a simple equal trade? He wasn't sure yet of the importance of his mistake in the overall game. Regardless, he hated making mistakes.

With the radio transmission Drozd knew that dead men tell no lies, but they also don't have the opportunity to confess. He was pretty sure that Dean was most likely guilty, but there was no hard proof yet. So now he was going to have to gather evidence to do just that. He had to prove that it was an ordinary crime of passion. *But was it?* He wanted to believe it could be that easy, cut and dry—jealous boyfriend, a fight, and an accidental homicide. But his intuition was telling him there was more to the story. *Why was the wound so neat? Where was she killed? Was there anything at Dean's apartment that would make this easy to solve?*

He needed to see the apartment for himself, so he got out of his car, locked the door, and headed toward the entrance of the stairs.

He walked up to Dean's apartment, and entered to see Officer Baker searching carefully to find any other clues related to Shelly's death. He looked around the room but saw nothing different from the night before except it seemed like Dean had cleaned up all the things that should have been taken out to the trash. There were multiple garbage bags lined up neatly in the kitchen waiting to go out. *What possessed him to deep clean before he died? Was that a clue? Did he have to tie up loose ends like he probably did with Shelly's body?* He snapped back from the thought as he approached Officer Baker. She was opening one of the drawers on a nightstand next to the bed.

Baker looked up and said, "Bill."

He answered, "Sue," like the acquaintances they were.

They had a mutual professional respect but nothing else. They had worked together before on multiple occasions, all small-town departments cooperated with each other.

Bill said, "Anything here that I should, see?" Sue replied, "Well, the note over there on the desk probably tells a bit of the story."

Drozd walked over to see a plastic bag sitting on the desk with the white piece of paper inside. He picked it up and read the note through the bag. It looked like it had been written with a shaky hand, and it seemed to sum up the end of Dean's life.

Drozd entered the bathroom to see the lifeless body of Gavin Dean. Officer White was still looking at the area surrounding the bathtub. Everything was neat except for the blood-tainted water in the tub. Dean's eyes were closed, and his face looked peaceful—no anguish evident. According to experts, this method of suicide was pretty painless. The person simply slit the arteries and the warm water just accelerated the blood flow causing death quickly like going to sleep. Experts say the hardest thing about this method is having the mental fortitude to cut deep enough into the wrists to sever those arteries. Many people who try simply cannot do it and end up in the hospital for treatment. Gavin Dean did it right.

Officer White pointed into the tub to the right side of Dean's body showing Drozd the outline of a razor blade knife. Later, they would discover the particular knife was produced by the company X-acto. The blade was definitely sharp and precise. Standing over the tub he looked at the walls around it. Nothing to see, no blood splatter, and no sign of a fight. The room was recently cleaned and smelled of Clorox bleach and what was likely a lemon-scented cleaning chemical.

"Anything else, Officer White?" asked Drozd.

White answered, "So far what you see is what you get, which is a whole lot of nothing. This looks like a straight up suicide, Bill."

Drozd agreed. On the surface it looked like it was all the proof he needed, but his intuition left him with doubts.

About fifteen minutes later the ambulance pulled up. They unloaded their equipment and gurney and proceeded inside and up the stairs. The State Police forensics team of Belle Vernon arrived around the same time and the apparent suicide scene became even busier. There was a lot of work to be done before Dean could be transported to the morgue. He would be in the same place as Shelly Lynn one last time. But this was not the ending that he had envisioned for them when she first agreed to go out with him at the Keystone Bakery.

Drozd, Baker, and White gathered up the evidence they had collected, including the note and Dean's phone and computer. His computer was an old PC-based laptop. They took everything and left the technicians and EMT paramedics to finish their work. The paramedics had removed Dean from the bathtub and were currently zipping him neatly into a black bag on the bathroom floor so he could be loaded onto the gurney and taken down to the ambulance.

Drozd was standing by the desk still looking at the note in the plastic evidence bag. He read each sentence out loud again and again. "I don't want to live without you. You deserved better."

Officer Baker said, "Sounds like the guy had a lot of remorse for something?"

Drozd replied, "But doesn't the wording sound a little bit weird? *You deserved better.*" Do you think he was talking about a better death or a maybe he should have been a better boyfriend?"

Baker looked up at him and stated, "It could really be either one, but it sounds like this guy is your killer."

Drozd said, "I'm going to follow up with Ms. Lynn. She said Gavin and Shelly had been having some trouble lately. I'd like to know what that was about. It might shed some light on the motive for the crime."

He watched the paramedics load the body on a gurney and start the process of getting the body down the stairs and into the ambulance. The coroner had declared the time of death as around 6:00 a.m. this morning so Drozd had assumed it was a long evening for Dean, contemplating his options and cleaning. In the end it seemed he had chosen the easy way out.

Drozd motioned for White and Baker to leave with him. They headed out the door and down the stairs, exiting into the late afternoon sunlight. They had spent the whole day going through everything time and time again. They tried to re-enact what must have happened to Gavin Dean. It all pointed to simple suicide. But they were left with questions. Why was the place clean? Why would someone who was so sloppy all of a sudden care what the world saw when they found his body? What did the note mean? The case just became more interesting to Drozd. He felt there was more to it, but he still hoped that it was a simple boyfriend kills girlfriend so he could watch the Steelers play on Sunday, maybe even spend time with Candice Collins, but it wasn't looking good.

CHAPTER SEVENTEEN

TOUGH CONVERSATIONS

He arrived at the house of Terri Lynn at around two o'clock in the afternoon the day after Gavin Dean committed suicide. It was the warmest part of the day, the temperature was around 70 degrees which, for Detective Drozd, was perfect. It had been an amazing fall in the Mon Valley.

Terri's house was aluminum-sided like many of the homes built at that time. Terri couldn't afford a brick house, which has many advantages during the cold winter months, but she did the best she could, and this was home.

When he walked up to the door, she was already opening it, her head leaning forward while she waved him in. She must have heard the car pull up. She invited him in, led him into the dining room, and told him to have a seat. He chose the chair at the far end of the table and sat down. She asked if he would like coffee ,and he politely accepted.

Returning from the kitchen with his cup of coffee, she gestured to the cream and sugar that were already on the table. He drank his coffee black so there was no need for any extras. He could see her eyes were swollen from a lack of sleep and all the tears that had been shed over the last 36 hours, which was quite understandable. Her one and only child was gone, and her world turned upside down with no chance of ever realigning itself. Drozd felt sympathy for her but he needed to do his job. He sipped his coffee, savoring its flavor.

Putting the cup on its saucer, Drozd said, "I know this is a horrible time for you, but I need to ask you some questions about the relationship between Mr. Dean and your daughter. Immediately he could sense the tension move into Terri's body, and he lost eye contact as she looked away. She sat back in her chair with a far-away look in her eyes.

"You told me that there might be some problems between them?" he asked.

She nodded slightly, and speaking slowly, said, "I only sensed it over the last couple of months," as her voice trailed off. "Shelly was tired of not being able to get ahead. I think she believed she would be further along at her age. Gavin tried hard but he was never going to have a career that afforded her luxuries."

Drozd asked, "So you feel she wasn't happy?"

"I think, to put it a better way, she was restless," she said, softening the harsh statement Drozd had made. "She seemed happier over the last three or four months though. She had some new clothes and shoes. I thought Gavin got a second job or somehow had been able to get a raise, but when I inquired, he just seemed to get irritated and quickly changed the subject."

"Did Shelly ever explain her new happiness?" asked Drozd, reaching for his cup of coffee to take a sip.

Terri stood up and replied, "No, and I didn't press the subject. Gavin didn't come here very often after I inquired about the possible raise. After that I thought it was best to let it alone, you know, let sleeping dogs lie."

Drozd pressed his brain to see the bigger picture, first processing before moving on. He asked, "So where do you think she was getting the items from?"

Terri replied, "Maybe she had a new acquaintance, but that would have been out of character for her."

Drozd was putting pieces together. New clothes, new acquaintance, maybe this was an easy case of jealous boyfriend kills girlfriend, then kills himself. That would be easy, logical, and clean. But the note said, "You deserved better."

Where was the gun? Where was the actual murder scene?

Drozd continued his line of questioning. "If Gavin wouldn't come here, then Shelly would have to be the one to go to visit him?"

Terri replied, "They would see each other three or four nights a week around his schedule. Sometimes Shelly would go out on her own, but I always thought she was just out with friends."

"But you're not sure and you didn't ask?" His fingers interlaced in front of him, his elbows on the table.

She shook her head no. Then tears started running down her cheeks and she started to sob.

Drozd knew this was the time to end their conversation, but asked if he could have a look at Shelly's room.

She replied, "Of course," and pointed him down the hall to a door on the left side of the hallway.

CHAPTER EIGHTEEN

"Big 21"

Dan Holiday wrote:

It was my twenty-first birthday. I had waited forever to legally go to a bar. My girlfriend and I, along with two friends, went to a bar with a band, and we were dancing, drinking, and enjoying the evening. The bar was big and there was a good crowd for a Friday night. The DJ was playing dance music, and the crowd was having a good time.

I had to go to the restroom but when I came back, I couldn't find my girlfriend. After looking all around I finally saw her slow dancing with another guy. They held each other close and swayed to the music. It sickened me. It was another example of not being the most important person to someone. My heart was broken. I just walked out the door and left. I got in my car and drove away. Why couldn't I be the center of her attention, just for one night?

Therapist Charlotte Burnett's reply:

Dan, did you confront this woman about her behavior? What was her explanation? Did she explain why she did what she did? What was the result of the confrontation? Did you continue in this relationship? It sounds like you were more into this relationship than she was. It sounds like you wear your heart on your sleeve. You gauge people by their actions and judge your worthiness based on those actions. Do you see this?

The killer thought to himself, *Doc, I just revealed the code, but you just don't understand.*

He stood and walked into another room. He was amused at how the game was progressing.

CHAPTER NINETEEN

Home Sweet Home

Detective Drozd entered Shelly's room and saw a tastefully decorated, understated space featuring light-colored furniture, all well aged. There were pictures of flowers in deep colors hung on the walls. *That might have been her taste or maybe her mom's*, Drozd thought. The bed was neatly made, the pillows arranged. The desk had a new iPad. Also, there were a few papers neatly arranged on the left side of the desk, *probably school assignments*, at first glance.

He moved to the closet which, for the most part, had items that were well worn in one section. But then he noticed, on the right side, the newer clothes. These clothes were obviously from a higher quality store and designer label, although Drozd himself had no idea who they were. It seemed like girls were concerned about clothes, bags, and shoes while boys were more interested in sports, cars, and girls, in his experience.

When he spotted the latest model Apple iPad on the desk, he wondered how she could afford such a luxury item on a clerk's wage. The iPad sat perched on a stand that held it upright and had a keyboard attached to it, in essence making it a computer, but there was a touch screen. Of course, it was locked with a passcode. He would ask Ms.

Lynn if she knew the code, but he wasn't optimistic because most people protected their privacy and didn't share the passwords for their devices.

In the bathroom he found the normal things but noted that some of the makeup was also from higher end stores you would find in the mall. For a woman who worked in a bakery, some of these items seemed a bit out of her financial reach. He needed to find out what the source of this new income was. He was sure the trail would lead to another party, the one who was providing Shelly Lynn the ability to afford some nicer things.

On her nightstand he found some magazines that featured many "models and celebrities." They were sporting some of the designer names labeled on the clothes that were tucked away in the corner of Shelly's closet. Where did the money come from?

Terri Lynn came to the door of the room and leaned against the door frame. Her eyes slowly scanned from side to side, observing every inch of the room. Surely, she was thinking about her daughter who she would never have the opportunity to share a conversation with again. He was sure she would have traded everything she had in this world for just one more chance to do just that.

Drozd asked, "By any chance do you know the passcode for her iPad? We recovered her iPhone but can't access either of them unless you know her passwords."

She responded, "0822, August 22—the day she met Gavin.

"May I take this iPad to the office temporarily to do a more thorough examination of the information on its drive? It might shed more light on what happened."

Terri asked, "Is that really necessary since they are both gone now?"

He responded, "Ms. Lynn, it's my job to find out, without a question, how your daughter was taken from you and by whom."

Grasping her mistake, she turned her eyes to the floor and responded, "Okay, I understand."

But what she really didn't grasp was that Drozd was going to cover all the possible angles of this investigation. He was looking at the chessboard and all possible moves. Then, and only then, would Terri have the true picture of what or who altered the life path of her daughter.

He carefully picked up the iPad, folded the keypad over, and walked out of the room toward the front door.

He said to Terri, "I'm sure I'm going to need your help further, so I'll contact you as soon as I have more information or more questions."

She nodded and watched as he walked out the door, back to his car.

He set the iPad on the passenger seat along with its charger and stand, started the car, and headed back to the office.

CHAPTER TWENTY

MURKY WATERS

Detective Drozd brought in Shelly Lynn's iPhone and iPad. He set them on his desk and walked away to pour himself a cup of coffee, black and hot. He was determined to find something, no, anything, that would jump start this investigation. He sat down and decided to open the iPad first.

He unlocked the iPad, and it came to life. The first thing he did was go through her social media. He had consulted some of the younger officers about these apps and how to navigate them. Facebook and Instagram didn't seem to reveal anything out of the ordinary. There were pictures of her and Gavin in various places around the valley, along with some random pics of her and some friends. He took note of a few of her girlfriends' names to see if they could shed some light on her life.

Next, he logged into her email account. It also didn't yield much. There were some advertisements from clothing stores and a few from Westmoreland Community College. When he opened the college emails, he noted they were reminders she was falling behind with her assignments, and one even stated she was going to be put on academic probation for the next semester if there was no improvement. He wondered why she was falling behind. Was it too much time with Gavin or something else?

He opened her Safari search and found a tab to a Hotmail account. It was left open and there were random emails from a website called LetsDoThis.com. On his own phone, he searched it and found what he was looking for— the source of her new improved financial landscape.

The site was a portal for "sugar babies" who were looking for "sugar daddies." The sugar babies were required to spend a certain amount of time with their daddy each month in exchange for a reward which could be monetary, or clothes, trips, rent, etc. The site contained pictures, descriptions, and a button to contact any of the women. He scrolled through page after page until he finally came across Shelly Lynn. It was definitely her, except her name was listed as Heather Rose.

He opened the emails with the subject line "You've been contacted." They contained a link to login, but it of course it pointed to the landing page where a username and password were required. There was no autofill and her normal username and password didn't work so he was locked out.

He wasn't sure how this worked but he was connecting the dots. Shelly had acquired extra money by spending time with men she met on this page. The emails began about five months ago, which coincided with the information Terri had provided. She said she started to notice the improvement in Shelly's financial status and her mood within that timeframe. It would also explain why her studies began to suffer. She must have been seeing these men at night, and it was interfering with her classes which were all night classes. She had to take night classes because she worked at the bakery during the day. *This was one very busy girl, between her classes, boyfriends, and a full-time job,* thought Drozd.

Now some tough questions were being answered. Drozd wondered if Gavin Dean's mood changed because he knew about this site. Maybe one of the men she met on the site was the killer. An angry client. His cut-and-dried murder-of-passion case had new questions to be answered. It still could be that Gavin found out about her indiscretion and mentally snapped. There were multiple possible motives now. He decided to focus on the opportunity part of the crime. Drozd needed to figure out where she was murdered. The bad news was he had no idea where it might be. This piece of the puzzle was first on his list, so he needed to dig deeper. He had many questions to answer but had to start somewhere.

He opened the iPhone next. Thank goodness it opened with the same password, 0822. This time it was her text messages that yielded what he was looking for. There were five unopened messages with just random phone numbers which were delivered over the last four days after she had been killed. But there was one opened text he noticed had come through the night of her murder around 8:30 p.m. That coincided with the end of her class and while she was having coffee with Gavin. Had he heard or read this text?

The text simply read "5M Hotel at 9:30." Now he had a lead on where the actual crime may have occurred. This case had just gotten more complex but at least the pieces on the chessboard were starting to have formation.

CHAPTER TWENTY-ONE

NO-TELL MOTEL

The 5M Motel was the typical no-tell motel that sported a giant pink neon sign in the parking lot and a row of rooms all on ground level. The motel specialized in an hourly-rate crowd. The parking lot allowed guests to pull in directly in front of their rooms and quickly enter, usually without anyone observing them, perfect for the 5M clientele. The motel had been around forever, and its seedy reputation was well known. It sat right along the interstate between Perryopolis and Belle Vernon. To get to it, one could exit off the highway and double back just a bit or come up the back road to the parking lot entrance.

It was a sprawling motel upon observation. In its day, it had been very busy with trucks traveling the interstate pulling off for the night to rest. But with the highway expansion the bigger chain hotels had moved into the area, taking business away from the older motels. At this point in time, the 5M Motel was more than willing to take any paying business it could get, including hourly, nightly, or even weekly. They asked very few questions of paying guests and even less if those guests paid cash.

When Drozd arrived, he surveyed the motel layout. He noted the entrance and exit. He could picture the cars pulling up and guests entering rooms without witnesses.

He parked and studied the establishment. He walked across the lot, opened the door, and entered the office which was located at the north end of the property. A bell sounded as the door opened announcing his arrival. A clerk exited a back room and approached the front desk ready to check in a new guest.

The clerk, who was also the owner, said, "Welcome to the 5M Motel. How can I help you?"

Drozd reached into his back pocket and unfolded his detective badge, showing it to the owner, saying, "Good morning, I am Detective Drozd from the Monessen Police Department. I need some information please," as he moved with purpose toward the desk.

Satisfied the clerk had seen his badge, Drozd put away his credentials, stating professionally, "I'm here investigating a crime that may have been committed at this establishment last week."

The owner, Sean Perry, took a step back from the counter uneasily responding, "You say a crime, Detective? I'm not aware of any crime committed here," tilting his head up, pursing his lips, and lifting his eyebrows.

Drozd asked, "May I speak with the person in charge here?"

Perry responded, "That would be me Detective. I'm Sean Perry, the owner of this fine establishment." He stood 5'8" tall with a slight build, probably weighing 145 pounds, not muscular, not fat, just average. Perry had blonde hair which was starting to recede but he kept the back longer, down his neck, and had light blue eyes. He wore a blue button-down shirt and jeans. His eyes were darting around nervously, especially now because Perry was busy calculating what crime the detective was inquiring about, there were so many that occurred regularly. There were drug deals, prostitution, and maybe a couple of other infractions at the 5M Motel, not to mention many moral indiscretions.

Perry owned the motel and had run it for the past 20 years, since his dad had taken ill and passed away. After his father's death he inherited it and had tried to do the best he could to keep it profitable, but economic times were tough in the Mon Valley. It had been the family source of income for over 60 years. In its day it had supported the family very well, but in the last 15 years, it had taken a drastic wrong turn. Now it had been reduced to a seedy, low-budget, end-of-the-road place to stop for whatever reason. Sean knew it would all be coming to an end soon, and he would have to find another way to make a living. The writing on the wall was simple, financially the motel was not providing the income needed to survive, and now, this trouble was going to be the last straw. He could feel it. But he was going to do whatever it took to continue this path as long as he could, so he readied himself for the detective's questions. If he could survive this bump in the road, maybe he could get another couple of years out of it.

CHAPTER TWENTY-TWO

VICODIN ES

Dan Holiday wrote:

*The woman I was with said not to return without
a prescription for pain medication or the pills
themselves. She had changed since the accident.
She accused me of cheating constantly. I had never
been unfaithful, but the most important thing in
her life at that point were the pills. She always said
she would quit and twice I had helped to bring her
down from the medication only for her to choose
it over me time and time again. For the most part
the pain had receded, but she chose the medication.
Why couldn't I be as important as it was?*

*I left the relationship by being unfaithful, which I
was extremely ashamed of.*

*But at that point I felt I could either die or save
myself.*

*Years later she called me and told me, I was
lucky to have been with her because she was out
of my league. I agreed with her and hung up. Two
weeks later she overdosed from pain medication and
passed away.*

Therapist Charlotte Burnett's reply:

Dan, an addict has a disease. Their brain chemistry changes from the medication. Their personality changes. It's not that you weren't important but more that she was sick. Yes, it sounds like she prioritized her love of the medication over your love but was it her fault? That's a question for her therapist. Unfortunately, it sounded like she hadn't gotten help for her problem. But you survived and became stronger from the experience. You removed a toxic person from your life when you had to. Your defense mechanism helped you survive.

It sounds more like your moral issue is with the fact that you saved yourself and couldn't save her. Do you think that might be possible? If so, do you think that act actually made you a bad person? Is it important to you to be thought of well?

The killer was now getting excited. Things were starting to move quicker and the plot was thickening. So far, he was right on target…no pun intended.

CHAPTER TWENTY-THREE

ROOMS WITH NO VIEW

"We believe that one of your rooms may have been used by a young lady who was involved in a bad incident last week, she was murdered," Detective Drozd said as he produced a headshot of Shelly Lynn to show Sean Perry. "Do you recognize her? We are following up all leads of places she may have been. We have credible information she met with someone here on the evening in question."

Perry's eyes shot open, and he looked up, saying, "Do you mean that is the woman that was on the news? When was she supposedly here?" he asked.

Drozd replied, "It was last Friday night, likely between the hours of nine in the evening and two o'clock in the morning. Can we look at your records of rooms rented please?"

Perry regained eye contact with Drozd, "Of course you can see them, but I personally check everyone in. I don't remember her being a guest. I would remember her. Her death was a tragedy," he said, trying to be convincing. But he was lying and not doing a great job of masking it. He had checked her in, she had paid cash. He thought it a bit strange that the key was just left on the bed the following morning and the room looked untouched. He certainly wasn't going to voluntarily give this information to the detective. He put his index finger to his mouth to appear as if he were thinking, but it was really to encourage himself to just be quiet.

"Maybe the gentleman checked them in and she joined him later," Drozd suggested. "I'm quite sure you don't watch all the rooms that closely, do you? There's an evident lack of security. I'm sure there have been a few indiscretions here from time to time, but that's not what I'm here for today. I just need to know who was here on the night in question. I can get a warrant, but you might not want that because all facets of your business will become public knowledge."

Perry spoke up right away saying, "Sure, detective, you can see my ledger, no problem at all! The only thing is all entries are done by hand because we haven't upgraded to a computer-based system yet." Perry also knew that Shelly had signed in under a male name. It was obviously not the real name of her companion. Perry didn't need this hassle right now. His brain registered that to appease the detective he would need to cooperate in some way. Maybe he could give him a little information, just enough to make him happy.

Perry produced a large book and opened it to the page for the Friday in question. There were six entries that night. He explained to Drozd that Fridays are not the biggest night for meetups because spouses were supposed to be home with wives and girlfriends. He went on to say that truckers are just finishing their haul and are eager to get home for the weekend.

The entries were almost comical: Joe DiMaggio, Fred Smith, John Wayne, to name a few. Drozd gave Perry a bit of a raised eyebrow and slight tilt of his head to make the owner squirm a bit. Both of these tactics were effective as Perry shifted his gaze away from him. There were at least three that warranted looking into, so he wrote down the names listed and any additional contact information Perry could supply.

Drozd asked, "I guess you don't make copies of their driver licenses or have any other information about these guests? What about payment receipts? I know I didn't see any security cameras when I arrived."

Perry raised his eyebrows in a quizzical look, but tried to look concerned replying, "Many pay cash and the less record of them being here the better they like it. Let's say I have adopted a bit of a 'no foul, no harm' approach to that. As far as cameras and video footage, it's the same thing. My guests really don't want a record of being here. So I look the other way because I really need their money."

Drozd asked, "Can you remember anything at all about those visitors?"

Perry decided to lead Drozd in a different direction since he knew it was indeed her that had checked in that evening. He responded, "I remember they were all guys, nothing special, just like any other night. It's hard to remember one day from another."

Drozd was seriously questioning Perry's truthfulness. He was starting to get annoyed, and he wanted Perry to know.

Drozd leaned on one leg, with his hand on his hip, and asked, "Can you at least remember what rooms were used that night by reviewing your incredible record ledger?" he said mockingly.

Perry squirmed a bit, looking away but then re-engaged Drozd saying, "I use the same rooms in sequence so the clients are the furthest away from the road and also my office. I can write that sequence down, or better yet, I can show them to you."

Drozd politely asked, "Can I please see those rooms?"

Perry replied, "Of course," as he turned around and reached for a master key that was stored in the drawer behind him.

CHAPTER TWENTY-FOUR

DAMN MAIDS

Drozd noted that all the rooms were mirror images of each other. As in most motels, the rooms have the exact same layout, right down to the furniture, color scheme, flooring, and even the linens on the beds and in the bathrooms. The design was outdated, a throwback to the 1980s, which was probably the last time this motel was truly prosperous. But one thing was for sure, they were clean! You could tell by the smell of strong industrial cleaning supplies hanging in the air. The cleaning staff must shampoo the rugs often, disinfect the sheets and linens, and scrub and polish the fixtures located in the bathroom because they sparkled. The decorating of the room left no lasting impression. There was a big sofa which was green, not plush or leather, just *green* described it best. The king-size bed sat in the corner of each room. They were covered in the normal drab white linens with a flowery comforter and pillows with white covers. And, of course, the obligatory bathroom stock of white bath towels, hand towels, and face cloths, all hung neatly, were present, all accounted for in number. All bathroom linens were well worn from years of laundering, and Drozd knew that no one was rushing to steal them from this motel.

Drozd looked carefully through each of those rooms.

Each was exactly the same, right down to the layout of where the furniture was placed. The only exception was in the next to last room he inspected. Just as he had done in the previous four rooms, he took his flashlight out and searched under the bed, finding nothing. But this time when he looked under the nightstand, one small thing caught his eye. Something in the corner reflected the light from his flashlight. When he retrieved it with a plastic-glove-covered hand, he discovered it was a small decorative pin with the insignia of California University of Pennsylvania printed on it. C-U-P was a small state college located in California, Pennsylvania, which was located about twenty minutes away. He had seen the logo before because a couple of years ago he dated a woman who had attended that college to earn her degree. He saw it on her certificate of diploma which hung on her wall, so it stuck out in his mind. Drozd bagged the pin and placed it in his front pocket. He wasn't sure if this was anything relevant. He couldn't even be sure this was the room where the crime occurred, but at least it was something. For all he knew the room may have been occupied by some college kids who were using it for a night of drinking and partying. Anything was possible.

Drozd would have sent forensic teams into each room but his budget was limited, and to make matters worse, the cleaning staff were very thorough. He wished they were a little worse at their job, it might have made his life easier.

After inspecting all six rooms and being satisfied that he had done the best he could, Drozd glanced one more time into the last room as he and Perry exited and locked the door. Drozd had come up with almost nothing at all except for the knowledge that Perry was hiding something and that he had found a decorative pin that probably was nothing. He made a mental note that if he needed to, he would return to squeeze Perry again to acquire more of the truth.

After sarcastically thanking Perry for showing him the rooms and helping him with the records, Drozd crossed the parking lot to his car and headed toward the interstate. He reflected on this chess game and concluded that his position in the game hadn't improved much with this trip. He was concerned that even this early in the match, winning the game was not a foregone conclusion, even though he was a good player. He hated to lose or even stalemate. He considered that failure, so he pushed it from his mind quickly and returned to work.

CHAPTER TWENTY-FIVE

HELPYOUNOW.COM

When Detective Drozd got back to the office he pinned the bagged evidence to his board in the upper right corner along with a small square of paper next to it with a question mark. He was not sure if it was actually a piece of evidence or nothing at all but he couldn't dismiss it.

He was also going to give Shelly Lynn's iPad another look today. Drozd walked across the room to his desk, picked it up, and unplugged it from the charging cable. He decided to look at the browser one more time when he came across HelpYouNow.com. What was that? How hadn't he seen this in his first examination? The login screen required a username and password. As he started to type, he thought this couldn't be as easy to get into. Could this woman be that much of a creature of habit? But to his amazement, the username and password were the same as her mother had provided him. The only place she didn't use the same combination, so far, was the Sugar Baby website. Being successful on three out of four attempts was an amazing average and he hoped his luck would hold up.

The screen identified that she had three new contacts from her therapist. They were from a therapist whose name was Charlotte Burnett. He felt a bit uneasy looking into her private conversations, but he had to follow up on all leads.

The therapist's emails were firm and unforgiving, exclaiming she was upset because Shelly hadn't checked in. She suggested she would prioritize the therapy session and that Shelly should call or text anytime. Their scheduled meeting was overdue seven days. Drozd knew that was exactly as long as it had been since Shelly had her life cut short.

He needed to get in touch with this therapist ,so he replied, "I'm sorry to tell you, but Shelly has been involved in a tragedy and has passed away. This is Detective Drozd of the Monessen Police Department. It's really urgent that I speak with you! Please call me at 412-555-1212."

He took a second to proofread his message and pressed send. He didn't know if he would hear back instantly or if would it be the next day since it was a Friday afternoon.

CHAPTER TWENTY-SIX

PATIENT-CLIENT PRIVILEGE

The call came the next day.

Therapist Charlotte Burnett spoke, "Hello, Detective Drozd, this is therapist Charlotte Burnett. I got your message late last night, and I waited to call until today because I had to gather myself after the news you gave me. Losing a patient is a really tough thing to put into perspective."

Drozd replied, "I completely understand, Ms. Burnette, especially when that life is taken away by someone else."

She interrupted, "Please call me Charlotte, and you are definitely correct about that. It makes you question why good people are sometimes taken early."

Drozd replied, "I'm Bill." Each was trying to bring the stress levels down a notch. "Charlotte, I need your help," he said respectfully.

"Bill, define what you mean by 'help,'" she asked with a little more tension in her voice. He replied, "I need you to discuss Shelly's sessions openly with me."

Charlotte quickly responded, "Bill, I'm not sure I'm comfortable doing that. I believe treatment is confidential. The privilege of speaking to someone on the deepest personal level is a responsibility to that person and their privacy, which is something I don't take lightly."

Drozd understood her conflict. He tried the personal approach next, stating, "Charlotte, I definitely think that Shelly was in trouble. I feel we owe it to her to put forth the very best effort to make sure whoever did this to her doesn't get away with it. The information you have is one of the few leads I have to go on." He further expanded his plea, saying "You may have information that could make the difference between catching this person or letting them get away with it, which would be a travesty. I personally want to hold that person accountable for what they did to Shelly and make sure they can never do it to anyone else, ever."

Charlotte paced her living room floor, weighing all the pros and cons of speaking candidly regarding her patient. She ran through all the legal ramifications. Next, she thought of Shelly and paused on the moral obligation she had to her. She was thoughtfully breaking things down until her checklist had its final answer. All of a sudden she stopped, stood up straight, and made up her mind. She had to help or she would forever know that her own moral guidelines got in the way of helping her client one last time. To her, that was unacceptable, so she committed to helping Drozd.

"Okay, I'm willing to speak about Shelly. First off, I want to explain that the therapy sessions I give are completed through a text portal. This means that I never get to see my client's face. This puts me at a great disadvantage for treating them effectively. I don't ever really know if the patient is lying or giving me truthful information. So what I am revealing to you could be true, half true, or just a plain lie."

Drozd said, "I understand and thank you for your honesty. I don't blame you for being skeptical of clients being one hundred percent honest with you during those text therapy sessions." Then softening his voice, he asked, "Why did she sign up for therapy?"

Charlotte said "I think Shelly was a bit lost in her life and it was stemming from guilt and remorse." She paused for a second and then continued, "Shelly had a boyfriend but she was also hiding some secrets. I don't think she had decided what her priorities in life were yet. I do know that she was torn over the choices she would have to make and the consequences that would result from those choices. It was causing great conflict within her belief system, and she felt great pain and inner stress."

Drozd said "Gavin was her boyfriend. He committed suicide two days after her death." He heard an audible gasp.

Drozd continued, "He left a note stating: 'You deserved better.' I'm trying to decipher what that meant. Was it better than him? Better things in her life? I'm just not sure at this point. But he was our main suspect up until he committed suicide. My first thought was that this was simply a crime of passion. But now I also come to find out that she was on a website whose main purpose was to put people together for paid secret relationships. Did she mention any of this to you?"

"She didn't come straight out and tell me she was being paid, but she did mention there was someone else that she was seeing. I can refer back through my notes, but I don't remember any specifics about him. I do know that Shelly was concerned about Gavin's emotional stability. She thought he was suspicious that she had something going on behind his back. His feelings put more burden on her and it was tearing her apart."

"So we can't rule out that Gavin might have found real proof of the affair, had a breakdown, and then committed this act?"

"I guess that is one plausible answer, but from what Shelly said, Gavin was gentle and caring. She did not really think he was capable of violence against her—she actually believed that he would harm himself if he found out. This was causing a great divide inside her."

The conversation went on for another twenty minutes but there was no further information that would lead Drozd in a different direction. He felt certain the murder of Shelly Lynn was committed by one of the two people they had discussed. Drozd gave her his email address and asked that she forward any information she felt pertinent. Then he thanked her for the conversation and repeated that she please contact him no matter how small or trivial the information was.

Burnett said, "Of course. Can you please keep me updated?"

He agreed, said goodbye, and hung up.

CHAPTER TWENTY-SEVEN

MURDER BOARD

The whiteboard hung on the north wall of Detective Drozd's office to the right of his desk, which was becoming less and less organized. It now had a growing number of pictures: Shelly Lynn, Terri Lynn, Gavin Dean, and now he had a black silhouette with a question mark on it. Was this a simple crime of passion with Dean temporarily losing his mind, killing Shelly, and then killing himself? Or was it someone else? Who was the mystery man who Shelly had been seeing on the side?

The therapist had confirmed this other person in Shelly's life. Why was the body placed so carefully? Why move the body? Where was the actual crime scene? Was it one of those rooms at the 5M Motel? If so, why weren't there any traces of the incident in any of them reported by the cleaning staff? Did that little pin have anything to do with this or was it just left behind by accident from a one-hour hotel resident?

His head was starting to spin. He needed a break from this case, so he took the afternoon for himself. He got in his car and drove to clear his head. His car sped down Highway 51 at 85 miles per hour. Highway 51 led straight to the bottom of the Laurel Mountains where he would test his engine with the steep ascent. He could see the exits located on the southbound sides of the steep road as his car bounded up the northbound lanes toward the summit. These exits were created for the large trucks moving cargo over the mountains which would sometimes lose their brakes on the way down the hill. The driver could use the turn off road to slow and stop their truck through the incline of the exit and the loose gravel composition. Many drivers owed their lives to these precautions. He himself never wanted to test them out. He continued up and stopped at the lookout spot that sat just below the summit of the hill. The view was breathtaking. On a clear day you could see 30 miles away. The mountains were covered in trees which, combined with the clear view in all directions, was nature at its best. He sat for quite a while thinking about nothing and everything. He was running the chessboard.

He needed to find information on this other man Shelly had been seeing. He decided his first course of action was to focus the next morning on just that. What made this murder different? A clean bullet to the head. It wasn't the normal "spray and pray" drug-related crime. It was a place to start.

The next morning he arrived at his office somewhat refreshed from his down time. He went into the database of unsolved murders in this area. He figured a 20-mile radius would be enough. He discovered that the records for Monessen and the surrounding areas only went back to the mid-nineties. The budget for digitizing crime information wasn't the same as in big cities like Pittsburgh and Philadelphia. This was little Monessen. But he checked anyway to see if anything fit.

Nothing caught his eye. *This is a dead end,* he thought as he spun a pen through his fingers with great dexterity and coordination. He had seen Val Kilmer demonstrating this in the movie, *Top Gun,* years and years ago. He plucked the pen from his fingers and put it between his lips resembling a dog guarding its prize bone. Returning to his keyboard, he expanded his search area to a 50-mile radius, stretching to the outskirts of Pittsburgh, located to the northwest of Monessen. Other slightly larger cities included Uniontown to the south, Washington directly west, and Somerset slightly southwest from Monessen. Their digitized records went back an additional decade since their populations provided a larger tax base and budget for law enforcement expenditures.

The computer paused for a moment before displaying a list of twenty-six unsolved murders between 1990 and 2013. He quickly scanned through the organized list. He rubbed his eyes and then checked again. There it was, his eyes weren't playing tricks on him. A small breadcrumb. Somerset, Pennsylvania, in 1993, there was an unsolved murder. The records listed the murder scene, a ski resort named Seven Springs. One male victim, Elliot Kidd. His cause of death was one gunshot from a .22 magnum bullet. No suspects. He clicked on the notes column and began to read through the crime scene information. Now he had something to work with. He just took an offensive position on the chess board.

CHAPTER TWENTY-EIGHT

SKI BUM

1993
Somerset, Pennsylvania

Elliot Kidd seemed like your usual ski bum hanging out at the lodge at Seven Springs Ski Resort. A long day of runs had left him cold, sore, and ready to be warmed up by the fire and to enjoy a spirit to warm his insides. The resort had received an amazing amount of snow in the last couple of weeks and more was predicted. He was determined to enjoy every run down the slopes over the next three days until he had to return to his monotonous job at the bank in Latrobe, Pennsylvania.

He had made branch manager three years before and although this was encouraging, the money just wasn't all that great compared to the huge salaries at the big city banks. The opportunities to move up the corporate ladder were few and far between at his bank. The job was monotonous and unrewarding and that's why he sought excitement in his life to balance it out. He looked forward to the challenging slopes but especially to his second favorite pastime, which was hunting snow bunnies to further warm him up. Tonight would be no exception, and he was excited to begin!

As he entered the bar his head swiveled from side to side, his eyes scanning for her. He didn't know who she was yet, but he was confident she would be there. His eyes stopped as he saw exactly what he was looking for. His first target was sitting at the bar in the lounge. The music was loud, the drinks were flowing, and this beautiful creature was the center of everyone's attention. Every man in that place wished she was with them. At 5'10", with straight jet black hair and green blue eyes, Lisa Lee was mesmerizing. She was part American, part Asian, giving her a unique appearance. She easily could have been a model. Elliot strode across the bar toward her. He knew that this girl was the exact challenge he needed for the evening and was up to the task.

Elliot was a very confident man, standing 6'1" with wavy brown hair and dark blue eyes. He prided himself on being fit, participating in sports, as a youth, at a high level, and now staying fit by playing tennis, swimming, basketball, and vigorous weight training. This gave him an edge for work and play. He knew that being handsome often opened up many doors not available to the not so fortunate, average-looking people.

Elliot walked up to the bar confidently and asked Lee, "Let me guess, Penn State class of 1991, right?" That would make her six years out of college or about 29 years old. This was perfect in his eyes. She glanced up, slowly turning her head to see who was speaking. She was getting ready to blow him off, not as gently as she normally did with most guys. But Elliot was not most guys, so she stopped for a second when her eyes caught his.

She took her hand and brushed her hair up on the side in a playful manner. With fire and life in her eyes, she taunted him saying, "Not Penn State, but you're close. Care to try again?"

Elliot put his index finger and thumb on his chin and tapped it playfully as if thinking.

He knew he would figure out the answer but why let on how smart he actually was. "Care to give me a hint?" he said with a slight smile forming, his straight white teeth now slightly exposed in a smile.

Women had deemed this a "mischievous" smile that had cut through many awkward initial moments with his conquests. He was aware of its effectiveness, and he always took full advantage of it.

With a bit of a playful tone in her voice she said, "You were partially right but answer this question: Who arrived in Massachusetts Bay Colony in the mid-sixteen hundreds? They were very religious."

Now she had him perplexed, which Elliot took as a good sign. She was engaged in banter. He racked his brain and suddenly it struck him like ringing a bell! His face lit up as he blurted out excitedly, "Quakers! You went to Penn!" It was extremely hard to contain himself. Victory was his as he complimented her by saying, "Wow, you have to be smart to survive that school."

Lisa was shocked that she had finally come across a man with something useful other than what was in his pants. She continued to flirt back. "You must have a brain to answer that one," she said, her turquoise eyes locking with his.

That was all he needed; they hit it off well the rest of the night. Drinks, conversation, and constant flirting, the trifecta for a perfect evening. But there was more to come.

When he suggested going back to his room and she accepted, he wasn't extremely surprised, but he was excited with thoughts of what was to come.

The night came and went as they pleasured each other again and again. Afterward, she simply got up, got dressed, and left. This was just the way he liked it, with no need for, *I'll call you,* or, *Let's get together again.* There was a mutual acceptance that they both had a good time, and then they parted with positive energy.

The next day he slept very late. Since he hadn't fallen asleep until after 5 a.m., he was exhausted, but in a good way. Late in the day he had recovered enough to ski through the night as he had done on two of the three nights he had been there so far.

Being a very proficient skier afforded Elliot some advantages. He could take some runs that weren't quite on the marked path but added ten extra minutes of run time. Seven Springs was good skiing by southwestern Pennsylvania standards but nothing close to the slopes of Colorado. The runs here were much shorter, so anything that added time was a bonus and worth the risk of getting caught by the ski patrol for late skiing or being somewhere you weren't really supposed to be. Better to ask for forgiveness than ask permission.

Snow was falling, and although visibility was low, the powder was perfect. Elliot was rounding a bend, leaning into the turn with the edge of his ski to decelerate just a bit when his ski caught, and he went tumbling forward coming to rest in the cold snow. No injuries, just embarrassment that he had apparently tripped on his own ski, or that's what he thought.

In a split second someone stepped out from behind a tree and before Eliot could stand, a silenced pistol was drawn and fired from no more than five feet away, striking Elliot in the head. He was dead instantly as the bullet entered his skull just slightly above his right eye.

The killer had done much work to track Elliot's movements through the first four days of his trip. This run was always on his routine because it was the most challenging. For the killer, though, it was the right spot due to how remote it was. He had spent much time finding that perfect spot where he knew Elliot would have to decelerate, guaranteeing the maximum effectiveness of the thin metal twine which was strung across the path.

Eliot was left at the foot of a tree resting peacefully. The snow, as expected, had covered his body and since he was skiing off the marked trails his body wasn't discovered until almost thirty-six hours later by the ski patrol search party.

The only way anyone knew to look for him was that his girlfriend, Julie, was worried because she hadn't heard from him in over a day and had called the resort trying to reach him. When he didn't answer the numerous calls to his room, they sent a security guard to check his room. The guard found his clothes still neatly hung but no sign of Elliot. The local police were called and a search was initiated since it had been more than 24-hours since anyone had seen or heard from him.

When they did find him, the snow had washed away all of the evidence and the killer was likely long gone. No motive, no evidence, little chance of finding the killer. One small bullet hole in the forehead the size of a dime and no blood.

CHAPTER TWENTY-NINE

Somerset

The Somerset Police Station was much nicer than the Monessen office. The same thought popped into Detective Drozd's head about taxes and law enforcement budgets. He quickly put that out of his mind and proceeded into the station.

Drozd identified himself to the desk clerk and then he was led back to the office of Lieutenant Graham Neff. Neff had been on the force for thirty years. He was pushing sixty but kept fit so he looked ten years younger.

Neff introduced himself, extended a hand, and continued, "Please call me Graham."

He asked Drozd to have a seat in the chair on the opposite side of his desk. Neff asked, "Detective Drozd, how can I be of assistance?"

"Graham, call me Bill, please. I am here because I'm looking into a case that happened about six days ago over in Monessen."

"Yes, I think I saw that on the news. Do you think it was drug-related?"

Drozd said matter-of-factly, "Usually that's what I get, but not this time. This time was something new. The reason why I'm here is that you have an unsolved murder from eighteen years ago that has a similar cause of death."

"That cause of death being?"

"A small gunshot wound to the forehead with the body seated against a tree. I read the crime reports but the actual investigating officer is not listed on your active roster so I contacted your office. Do you know Detective Nard?"

Lieutenant Neff pulled back slightly at the mention of the question. He regained his composure quickly and sullenly said, "I did know Jeff. He passed away about seven years ago from cancer. Great man. Good detective. Gone way too soon."

Drozd was sad to hear this, and he slumped back in his seat. "Were you here back then?"

"I was, but I wasn't around the case. I know Jeff lost a lot of sleep over that one. There just wasn't any evidence. It looked like a Mafia assassination. Definitely professional and executed with some skill. Creepy the way the body was posed."

Drozd interjected, "Same thing with our victim. Other than a small hole in her head, she could have just been resting. Were there any notes left from Detective Nard or just what was in the crime notes?"

Lieutenant Neff said in a somewhat defeated tone, "What you have read in the online file is everything I have. I'm sorry. I wish I could have been more help. I'm sure Jeff would have had more insight.

Drozd frowned and realized he had hit a brick wall. Two steps forward, one step back, he thought. He felt he had lost a piece from his chess board, but the game wasn't over by any means.

CHAPTER THIRTY

Burning the Candle

Detective Drozd arrived back to the office around 5:30 that afternoon. He had stopped and had a bite to eat because he knew it was going to be a long evening. He poured himself a cup of coffee, not the freshest cup, but caffeine would be his best friend for the long night ahead.

He was running the scenarios. Mafia-style killing. Professional. No trace evidence. What was the motive? What was the means? Shelly was cheating on Dean. Was Elliot Kidd, also cheating? That case was so old that there wouldn't be witnesses left to interview. A dead end in the chess game.

He decided to go back to the drawing board. He needed to contact the website where Shelly had been advertising her services.

Let's Do This made it almost impossible to contact them. They were based in Switzerland, and everyone knows about how the Swiss view their privacy, evidenced by their banking systems rules. Eventually he found a contact email address. In his message he introduced himself, and requested someone please contact him in regards to a murder investigation in the United States. He wasn't holding out much hope for them to get back to him quickly. He would be right.

He backtracked and checked firearms records for .22 caliber magnum handgun registrations in the area and found there are around 13,000 of those guns in southwestern Pennsylvania and about 160,000 of that general model in the United States. Talk about your needle in a haystack.

He decided it was time for the deep dive. He had been to the library of Monessen early this morning and requested the microfilm of the *Valley Independent* newspaper dating back to the seventies. The administrator, Fred, was happy to help Drozd because he was familiar with the story about the recent murder of a young lady. Drozd arrived at the library around 7:30 and the desk clerk was waiting with big boxes and a microfiche film reader.

He sat in his office bleary eyed. It was 2:14 in the morning. He had started scanning every day of every paper starting on January 1st 1980. He was almost through the 80's when he discovered something on April 14, 1988. He came across an article buried toward the back of the paper about an individual killed in what was determined to be a drug deal gone wrong. One thing caught his attention. There was a bullet wound in the victim's forehead. It wasn't exactly a perfect match because there were also multiple shots to the victim's chest, but it at least warranted further looking into.

CHAPTER THIRTY-ONE

MEET AND GREET

1988
Donora, Pennsylvania

The drug dealer waited in the back parking lot of the run-down, abandoned office building. It was spring so things were starting to warm up a bit but the evening temperatures still hovered in the low 40s. The building, which used to house a construction company, was located well out of the way of the more populated areas, sitting at the end of a dead-end road. The streetlight directly in front of it had burned out long ago. Due to the buildings location, few people ever ventured there because it was dangerous, especially after dark. The building had been empty for a couple of years due to the owners refusal to pay for all the necessary repairs required to meet city codes, and the business had closed long ago when the steel mills moved out. So it sat empty but provided a perfect place for the drug dealer to deliver his product to buyers.

The car drove up, stopped, and a man exited. Danny waved a hand at him and said, "About damn time, man. It's fucking cold out here!"

The man from the car simply shrugged, as if not really paying much attention. Danny looked down as he reached for the drugs which were in his right front pocket. But as he did, a gun was drawn in one smooth, quick move and a shot was fired at close range, hitting Danny in the middle of his forehead. He dropped to the ground, dead on impact. The killer proceeded to fire repeatedly into Danny's chest until he was out of bullets. Then he walked the area accounting for all the shell casings from his work. He opened the trunk, picked up the body and put it in, closed it, and drove away.

Danny's body was found by the side of the road, under a tree, off of Highland Avenue in Donora, Pennsylvania. Donora is a borough of Monongahela which is located along the Monongahela River. The town was always known for its drug problems due to the economic inequality in the Mon Valley.

Danny Johnson was twenty-four years old and had long been involved in selling illegal drugs—mostly speed and marijuana—but he had also been known to have a wider variety available on occasion. He had been in and out of trouble with the authorities since a young age. In high school he had a brief stint competing on the Ringgold football team as a wide receiver, but he had been suspended from the team due to his low grade-point average. Once he left the team, he never made an attempt to return.

Danny never recovered from being suspended from the teams which contributed to his becoming an angry man. He felt like the writing was on the wall for him, so he soon resigned himself to becoming the official drug supplier of the same football teammates he trained with and competed alongside. They were anxious to purchase his products, along with many other shady characters in the area. He always said "You have to do what you have to in Donora."

CHAPTER THIRTY-TWO

HANGOVER

Detective Drozd went home for about four hours to sleep and shower. He made coffee although he thought his blood was still caffeinated from staying up nearly 24 hours. He felt hung over because sleeping for three hours didn't offer much of a recovery, but the shower and large cup of coffee cleared the fog.

He drove back to the office and observed his murder board with a clearer mind. He had to research the small breadcrumb he discovered the night before—the murder of Danny Johnson. To do so he needed to see if anyone recalled the crime, so he called the Donora, Monongahela police office, identified himself, and explained what he needed. The desk clerk thought for a moment about who could help and then suggested that Commander Kapty was the one to speak with. He put Drozd on hold then returned stating that Commander Kapty could see him if he could be there by 11:00 that morning. Drozd thanked him and hung up. He had an hour and a half to recheck his notes on the murder one more time.

At 10:15, Drozd started making his way to Donora. The drive took Drozd along the river, and to his right there were large cliffs. At a quick glance they were beautiful with their jagged edges and formations. The rivers carved the winding path of the Mon Valley over the course of time.

When constructing one of the roads many years ago, workers found dinosaur bones as they cleared areas of these rock formations. Although the rock formations were beautiful to observe, they were hazardous. There were often rockslides as the cliffs shifted and gave way, crashing to the road below. Many times the road was blocked until it could be cleared by large construction vehicles.

He turned left and crossed the old metal bridge. It was a miracle that half the bridges in the area weren't collapsing. They were all very old, built in more prosperous times when the steel mills flourished and the tax base could support construction of the infrastructure needed. He drove through Donora, passing dirty, dingy, and run-down homes and small businesses. The same road led to Monongahela which, by contrast, was a much cleaner, tidier city. The residents earned higher incomes than poverty-stricken Donora. He arrived at the police station at 10:53. Drozd was always early. He thought it was disrespectful to be late so he made it a point to never be.

Inside he presented his credentials and told the desk clerk that he was supposed to see Commander Kapty. He was shown back to his office where he introduced himself. Commander Kapty was a stout man in his early sixties. He had gray hair and intense brown eyes that demonstrated the seriousness of his demeanor. He was cordial, waving Drozd into his office.

After exchanging some short pleasantries Drozd said, "Commander, I'm here to see if I can get any information about a cold case that took place back in the late 80s in Donora." Drozd knew that this station covered law enforcement in both towns.

The Commander raised an eyebrow and said, "That's quite a while ago detective."

Drozd nodded in acknowledgement and told the Commander about how he had come across the article in the *Valley Independent* about the murder and some of the general details. He continued explaining that his interest was in the bullet to the forehead and not so much the other shots to the torso. He described his current investigation and the similar way the victim had been shot in the head. Drozd knew it was a stretch but at this point he was following up all leads possible.

Kapty said, "But why would you think this was the same person committing crimes so far apart? 1988 to 2013 is a long stretch of time. That's 25 years, if my math is correct."

"Spot on, Commander, but I also have an unsolved murder that happened up in Somerset back in 1993. It had the same cause of death, which was a small caliber shot to the head at close range, and then the body posed under a tree."

Kapty scoffed in a dismissive tone, "Are you insinuating there might be a serial killer in this part of Pennsylvania? We've never had one of those as far as I can remember."

Drozd spoke with a matter-of-fact tone, his left arm reaching back, scratching the back of his neck, "Commander, I'm not sure what I have. You know my case could still simply be a matter of boyfriend gets mad at girlfriend and ends her life then offs himself a couple of days later. But I want to be thorough in my investigation to have the best chance of closing my case. You know, crossing my t's and dotting my i's to make sure I've done the best job I can. With that being said, at this point, there are some things I'm still trying to wrap my head around that don't make sense."

"Well, what can I do to help you?"

Drozd sat up, and his focus kicked in as he asked, "Do you personally have any recollection of this murder?" Kapty sat back in his chair a second, thinking back. He stated, "I remember it vaguely, but I don't have any specific recollections. It was just so long ago. I'm sorry I can't be of more help."

"Maybe you still can. I know you don't have archived digital records of murder investigations but what about written ones?"

"Of course."

"Can I please use them to research any information that might help with my case?"

"Of course, my boy," and quickly picked up his phone. He called the desk clerk and explained what he wanted and within one minute that clerk showed up to escort Drozd to the case archives.

"Good luck with your case, Detective."

"Thanks for the hospitality, Commander."

The desk clerk led Drozd to the basement.

CHAPTER THIRTY-THREE

THE LAND DOWN UNDER

The basement was three flights down. The room was huge. Over 100 feet long and 15 feet wide, with 13-foot ceilings. It was brightly lit with florescent bulbs. The air was slightly thicker with a touch of humidity. It was very quiet and reminded him of a library. It would be a good place to work and concentrate, he thought. The sheer amount of data stored here was impressive. There were rows and rows of metal shelving that backed up against all walls and more rows in the middle of the room. The shelves had boxes dating back into the 1960s, organized by dates. The oldest boxes were located on the far back right side of the room.

Detective Drozd thought, *This is going to be a long process to find one cold case file.* But the clerk helped Drozd find the boxes containing files from the 1980s. There were still hundreds of boxes that could contain the file he was searching for, but, once again, the clerk came to the rescue by narrowing down the search area dedicated to the late 80s. Drozd started checking all the names on the boxes one at a time. What he thought was going to take days was actually about an hour and a half. He finally came across what he was looking for—a box labeled "Danny Johnson April 1988." Drozd reached for the box and noticed it had a light layer of dust on it. He thought, nobody was actively trying to close this case.

Drozd wiped the dust with a quick swipe of his hand and then carried the box all the way to the other side of the room where there were three desks set up for reviewing evidence. The box was light, and he assumed that it was not filled with many documents. Inside it he found two file folders that were very thin. One was labeled, "Danny Johnson Background" and the other "Case 1962."

Drozd first examined the Johnson folder. It contained records of his arrests, accusations, and general facts about his life including his family, addresses, and names. Well, this gave him a pretty clear picture of who Johnson was: a typical drug dealing street thug from what the records indicated. What might he have to do with Drozd's case?

The other folder, "Case 1962: was sparse. It consisted of four pages including the autopsy and some pertinent facts about the case. The lack of paperwork was a testament to how little effort was put into solving Johnson's murder.

Drozd read through the paperwork which contained the details about the case. It was a basic crime scene form.

It read:

> **Daniel Johnson**, Age 24
> **Time of Death:** Between 10:00 in the evening and 1:00 in the morning, either April fourteenth or fifteenth, depending on the actual time of death.
> **Cause of death:** Gunshot wound.
> There was a diagram of a body with the location of the shot circled and a scatter diagram of the many shots to his midsection.
> **Murder weapon:** .22 caliber magnum handgun.

Notes: Body had been moved from original scene to discovery location. No exact crime scene identified.
Victim's surviving relative: Mother, Gerry Mae Johnson.

It identified her residence in the projects of Donora. It had a contact number which Drozd wrote down along with other pertinent information.

He sat back in the chair and thought, *They definitely didn't put much effort into solving your murder, Danny.*

He made copies of the documents. After he returned the original pages to their respective folders, he returned the box to the shelf. He returned to the main floor, gave the desk clerk a wave and left to drive back to the office. His next step would be to contact Gerry Mae Johnson later in the day.

CHAPTER THIRTY-FOUR

MY BOY

Detective Drozd drove up the hill into the projects. He was surprised that Danny Johnson's mom still resided there, but it could be a very hard road to get out.

He parked outside Building D. Pulling out his notebook, he double-checked the apartment number before venturing out. It was a pleasant day. The sun was out, the humidity low, and a slight breeze came from the northeast. His notes read, *apartment 16, Building D*, and soon he found the right place.

It took a few minutes for someone to answer, although he heard stirring right away. The woman inside peered through a peephole and asked, "Who is it?"

"Detective Bill Drozd from the Monessen Police Department, ma'am," he said. "We spoke on the phone yesterday in regards to your son Danny. May I come in and speak with you please?"

She unlocked the door and opened it, allowing the sunlight to enter, along with fresh air. She shielded her eyes for a moment while her pupils adjusted. Gerry Mae Johnson very rarely ventured out into the sun these days. Her mobility was limited, and she looked tired and worn out. She guided him in and gestured for him to sit in a chair in her living room. She looked nervous but that could have been due to her lack of social interactions these days.

"How can I help you detective?" Gerry Mae asked in a frail, raspy voice, caused from years of chain-smoking cigarettes. Her body was giving up. She had problems breathing and her blood circulation had diminished. She wasn't very old but, even with the help of modern medicine, there wasn't much that could be done to help her.

Drozd said, "First, Ms. Johnson, I'm so sorry for the loss of your son. Losing a child has to be the hardest thing in the world. I don't think that the truth was discovered in regards to your son's death. Maybe, between you and me, we can try and right this and get more answers about that night. Can you tell me what you remember about the night of his death?"

Gerry Mae responded quickly, "You mean his murder? Why now after all this time?" Drozd could tell this was a very sensitive topic for her.

She didn't expect a response from him. She calmed down and said, "Listen, Detective, Danny was no saint. It's likely he was doing something that he shouldn't have been doing, went someplace he shouldn't have gone to that night, and was doing God knows what! The only thing I can't understand is why he was shot down like a dog and left under a tree on that street on display!"

Bam! There it was! This fact—found under a tree— wasn't listed in police reports Drozd had reviewed. He had information about it being the same caliber gun. He saw the location of the gunshot, along with the spray of other shots to the body. But neither the newspaper nor the police reports mentioned he was under a tree. This was a small success proving his theory about a serial killer being involved. He didn't want to let on to Gerry Mae that this was a big deal so he returned to her statement that her son "shouldn't have been shot down like a dog."

Drozd regained his calm disposition even though his adrenaline was spiking. He agreed with her in regards to how her son was left. He then followed up by asking, "Did you see him on the night of the murder, and if so, was there anything strange about his behavior?"

"I saw him for dinner. Nothing different. He said he had to go meet someone but he didn't say who. I usually knew what that meant. You know—wrong place with the wrong person, doing the wrong thing kinda situation."

Drozd had his hands flat to his sides and had sat up a little bit straighter. "So nothing, not even something small, that you might have thought was insignificant at the time?" he asked.

"Nothing that I recall. I'm only sorry that nobody cared that my son died. The police didn't even try to find his killer."

Drozd empathized with her. If it were his child, he would have reacted the same way. He said in earnest, "I understand, ma'am. I'm going to try hard to help you and maybe I'll get lucky. If I find out anything I'll let you know. If by chance something else comes to mind, here is my contact information."

Gerry Mae accepted the card and nodded. She asked if he could see himself out as it was hard for her to get around.

He stated, "No problem."

Drozd went out the front door, taking care to make sure it was fully closed. Returning to the car he felt badly for her. Here was a mother who had a double-edged sword in front of her metaphorically. She didn't know what actually happened that night and maybe it was better that way. At the same time she knew who her son was and that had to be tough. But the hardest thing she faced was the simple acceptance of the fact that her son probably made just one mistake that night, which cost him his life.

Driving back to Monessen, Drozd was running down his whiteboard diagram in his mind. It was a twenty-minute drive. He had plenty of things to add. He felt he had turned a corner and taken a superior position on the chessboard!

CHAPTER THIRTY-FIVE

Class Act

When Detective Drozd arrived back at the office there was a Post-it note attached to his computer screen reminding him to return a call to therapist Charlotte Burnett. He immediately picked up his phone and dialed her number. She picked up on the third ring, so he assumed she was not in a session at the moment.

She had seen the phone number on her screen and knew it was a call from him. He excitedly said, "Hi, Charlotte, Detective Drozd here. I got a message to call?"

"Wow, a quick reply, Bill. It's not typical for a man to call back quickly," she playfully said. She had no idea why she had just said that, but he had a nice way about him and gave off a good vibe, so she went with it. She wondered what he looked like, but she would worry about that later. She recovered and said, "I got a chance to review my notes from our sessions, and Shelly did mention something about school in regards to him."

Drozd was taken aback for a moment, and kind of excited at the same time when Burnett seemingly flirted with him at the beginning of the conversation. He reclined back in his seat with his arms above his head, the phone cradled in between his neck and shoulder, stating, "I already know that her boyfriend went to the same school she attended."

Charlotte corrected him, "No, no, not her boyfriend. I'm talking about the other person she was spending time with. Maybe the fact that she knew that they might cross paths was a stressor and maybe she thought they might be discovered."

"Doesn't make sense. You know the website she was on was maybe not straight up prostitution but it certainly was a sugar-baby arrangement."

Charlotte asked, "Sugar-baby?"

A bit sheepishly, Drozd said, "You know, it's a paid relationship with benefits. It's a one-on-one arrangement. It's different in that not just any stranger can pay for time with the girl. The girl can choose the one person she wants to start a relationship with. I sincerely don't think that there are many college students that could afford to supplement the income of a sugar-baby. But I'll follow up on this information. I can take a ride over there and see if I can find anything."

"Couldn't hurt," Charlotte conceded. "I'm sure something will turn in your favor soon. I would love to give you something more to catch this creep, but I figured anything, even something vague like this, might help. I'll keep thinking through all of this, and if there's anything else I think of, I'll let you know," she said with a positive tone of conviction to her voice.

Bill decided to flirt back to see if he could get any signals. "And I promise I will call quickly anytime you want," he responded. He drew out the word "anytime" and they both started to laugh. "Anyway, thanks for the information," now sounding more professional again.

He hung up the phone, sat forward in his seat, and started spinning the pen feverishly through his fingers. His mind felt sharper now. At the same time, he started thinking about relationships and about Charlotte Burnett. He liked the response he got when he flirted back. He wondered what she looked like, but he would worry about that later.

CHAPTER THIRTY-SIX

CHEATING 101

Dan Holiday wrote:

Girlfriends have always cheated on me. I have never understood why but, at the time, I guess being open to dating multiple people was the trend. It would have been fair had that been the guideline laid down in the beginning, but for me it wasn't. One girl cheated on me multiple times. She did it once and when I found out I ended up taking her back. Several months later she did it again. It shook me to the core. My outlook on relationships has never changed since then. I guess I couldn't figure out why they did it. I treated them well but there wasn't a reciprocal moral code for them to treat me well by being faithful.

Therapist Charlotte Burnett's reply:

Dan, I can hear the pain through your words. It is incredibly hard to go through a situation like this. Going through it multiple times is awful. You seem to wear your heart on your sleeve and leave yourself open to this. Why do you think you tolerated it more than once? Do you feel like you were unworthy of them being faithful? Did you confront this person about their behavior? Did they have an excuse? It sounds like these events might be a root in what we discussed earlier, in regards to your lack of self-esteem and why you are non-confrontational.

How do you deal with situations like this now? We have some work to do to rebuild your self-esteem. You are a good person and you have to learn to remove these toxic people from your life.

Dan Holiday sat back at his desk and scratched his head. He chuckled a bit and said, *Doc, if you only had a clue how I remove people. I'm going to give you a chance to see it in person someday...very soon.*

CHAPTER THIRTY-SEVEN

WCC

The college was very small. The students were low-income kids who didn't have the grades or money to attend large universities. For those less privileged, it was a start in the right direction. Detective Drozd entered the building and proceeded to Dean Marty Stranko's office. Stranko was a slightly pudgy man who, from Drozd's first impression, seemed an upbeat, positive individual. He was well liked among the students and faculty and he cared for everyone.

In the outer office, Drozd was greeted by Paula Beck, the assistant to Dean Stranko. She took Drozd back to the office, and Drozd noticed Stranko had a sad look on his face. He extended his hand to Drozd and said, "I've been expecting you. I assume you're looking for any information I can provide about Shelly and Gavin? First off, I want to extend my condolences to their families. I can't imagine what they are going through. The last couple of days have been horrible on the students and faculty. We have counselors temporarily on staff to assist anyone who is having difficulty dealing with their deaths. We are all in shock."

"That would be helpful, sir. Any insight might help."

Stranko said "They both were good students and well liked from the comments I am hearing. They were together often. They shared a couple classes. I don't think they had many friends because, if I'm not mistaken, they both worked full-time jobs on top of their class load. I like that because it shows they were taking responsibility for their own lives. Unfortunately, that's pretty much what I can offer. I wish I had more I could share with you. I feel really helpless. You know I have hundreds of students here and often I can't get as close to them as I'd like."

"I understand sir. In order to help gather more background and get a clearer picture of them, can I please see their class schedules and by chance can I have permission to speak with their teachers and maybe some of the students somewhere here on campus today instead of asking them to come to my office?"

Without hesitation, Dean Stranko replied, "Of course, I'll get their schedules and set up some times for today for teachers to speak with you. I'll put you in a small office down the hall. Anything else that I can do to help?

"No, sir, what you are providing will definitely aid with the job I have in front of me. Thank you very much."

"Anything to help our kids."

Drozd believed the sincerity in his voice. He seemed like a good, caring man.

The rest of the afternoon was spent speaking with the professors and getting a sense of any changes in their grades, interactions, and mannerisms. He took diligent notes and tried to gauge if anyone knew anything about someone besides Gavin that Shelly might have been interacting with more often. He also had the Dean assist him in finding a couple of the names that he had acquired from Shelly's Facebook account. These friends all said that Shelly and Gavin were an amazing couple. They believed they would get married and live happily ever after. None of them seemed untruthful when Drozd gently tried to suggest that Shelly might have had another boyfriend. In fact, they seemed truly surprised when he brought it up.

Although not fruitless, there weren't many clues that might lead him to the identity of this other person of interest. He returned to his office a bit defeated because the day was unproductive. He didn't end up with much to show for his work, just a few confirmed facts he already knew.

The highs and lows of the game, he thought. *Maybe tomorrow would be a better day.*

CHAPTER THIRTY-EIGHT

A BIGGER NET

Detective Drozd leaned back in his chair with his hands above his head. He was spinning the pen through his fingers rapidly, staring at the murder whiteboard. He was considering all the facts over and over again, trying to navigate the maze, but he kept hitting a dead end. He thought the three murders were connected, but he wasn't positive about that yet. He knew there still was a chance that Shelly's boyfriend might have killed her in a crime of passion. But that wasn't what his intuition told him. It was telling him there was much more to this, and usually his instincts were correct.

He thought about what he had accomplished so far. He had found the three murders through records of both law enforcement and public access. He couldn't contact every police department or look at every newspaper distributed across the country for the last twenty-five years to dig deeper. He thought about what he could do to narrow his search. He came up with an idea. He knew he was going to need help. The Federal Bureau of Investigation might be the answer. The federal law enforcement databases could contain answers. If he found the right connection within that agency who was willing to help, maybe they could close his case and solve the other cold cases.

So far the timeline had murders in 1988, 1993, and 2013. There was a five-year time gap in between the first two but then nothing until twenty years later. What if there were more murders during the years in between those time markers, or even before 1988? The FBI has searchable databases that cover the entire country. The best part was he remembered those records dated back to the late 1970s. Maybe the haystack he was searching for these needles in had just gotten a little smaller.

He picked up his phone and dialed the number of a contact he had made back when he was working in Columbus, Ohio, at his prior job. The FBI agent's name was Carlos Sanford, and he had been helpful in the past when Drozd had reached out to him. He hoped it would be the same result this time.

FBI Agent Carlos Sanford answered on the second ring. "Agent Sanford here, how can I help you?" he asked.

Sanford stood 5'9" and weighed 170 pounds. He had brown hair and brown eyes. He was a very fit man in his early fifties but easily could have passed for being in his forties. He had very little body fat. He had loved the daily workouts when he was in the armed services, and in the FBI physical fitness was also the foundation of productivity. Their approach was simple: sound mind, sound body. That emphasis on his mind and body had helped Sanford excel in whatever he did in his life. Having grown up in Los Angeles, in the suburbs of Burbank, he had joined the armed services after high school and finished two tours of active duty before using his military benefits to attend college and graduate with his degree. He had excelled in his studies and was ranked high in his graduating class at UCLA. After college, the combination of honorable service in the military and his advanced degree had fast tracked him into the FBI training program. Since then he had become the leader of a team of data analysts.

Drozd said, "Good morning, Agent Sanford, Detective Drozd from the Monessen Police Department here. I'm not sure if you will remember me, but we collaborated on a case years ago when I was employed by the Columbus Police Department."

Sanford said, "Oh, yes, I do recall our past work Detective Drozd. Wasn't it that missing person case a while back?"

Drozd replied, "Spot on, sir. We solved that one, but it wasn't easy. I could never have done it without your help. Thank you again."

Sanford replied, "No need for thanks, that's what we do." He continued, "What are you into now, Detective?"

Drozd laid out all the facts, starting with the murder of Shelly Lynn, explaining the cause of death, strange crime scene, and how out of the normal it was, in his experience. He shared the 1988 murder of Danny Johnson, explaining that this murder had a variance with extra gun shots to the chest. He ended with the murder of ski bum Elliot Kidd, who had a consistent cause of death. All three had been moved after they were murdered and posed at the bottom of a tree. He explained he wasn't exactly sure if the Lynn murder was a crime of passion, but the posing and the way the victim's wound had been cleaned up had him leaning toward there being another person of interest.

"Uh-huh…sounds like some bad stuff. Too many coincidences in your facts not to take notice. I don't believe in coincidences. But now to the million dollar question— how can the FBI assist?"

"Does the FBI have crime databases that encompass the U.S.? If so, there may be more murders that are similar with the ones I have uncovered so far. I got extremely lucky in finding what I have up until now, but my luck has hit a wall. I need a way around that wall, and I think your agency can help."

"So you think there might possibly be a serial killer out there who has acted in your area, but also think, because of the holes in the timeline, that he may have acted in other areas of the country?"

"Well, it's possible, sir. I'm just working the case. The facts are there are three murders that may be linked. Two happened within five years of each other and then there was a fifteen-year gap between the second and third murders. Why would the murders stop and then start again? I guess there are many possibilities like jail, sickness, moving, or a million others that would explain it, but through all my research and experience I have found that once a serial killer starts to hunt, they don't usually stop. They simply get better at what they do."

"So if I do a search for crimes with similar circumstances and find some, are we now working together as a team? I don't want to take over your case, and I'm sure you don't want that either, but a cooperation of our resources could be beneficial to both of us."

"I don't care who finds this guy, sir. I need to find him, stop him from doing it again, and put him away forever. That's the only acceptable outcome."

"Okay, send me over all the research you have so far. Then make me a list of keywords you think might narrow down the search parameters for my team. We can see where that takes us. Do you have my email address on file to send that data to me?"

"Yes, sir, I do. And let me say I look forward to working together again very much."

After they disconnected Drozd started uploading the files and emailed them to Agent Sanford. He felt with more eyes on the chess game he could move faster and become more aggressive.

CHAPTER THIRTY-NINE

ONE SMALL STEP FOR MANKIND

The room was alive with multiple computer monitors. Agent Sanford was overseeing their progress. He had assigned each of his team a job. They were headquartered in Washington, D.C., at the main offices located in the J. Edgar Hoover Building.

Sanford had risen through the ranks with exemplary work through attention to detail and demonstrated an advanced level of managing people. This wasn't easy to accomplish, but he excelled by adhering to certain management- and training-style guidelines.

On the first day new trainees arrived, he informed them that the day they started working for him was the first day of their career as far as he was concerned. This relieved any pressure the person had and allowed them to start fresh. Everyone started at the same level no matter what their prior experience or inexperience consisted of. He wanted to train them to do the job as a team not as individuals.

He also told them they were capable of achieving more than they ever thought they could. He used the example of the U.S. Census Bureau's household information program, tasked with gathering population information biannually determining density and other demographics of all regions of the country. When they switched over to the computer punch card system to be more efficient, all new trainees were told that punching data on 250 cards per day defined success. It was no surprise that within a reasonable amount of time all staff reached that goal. The next time the Census Bureau's work needed to be done, the same staff members were challenged by management to punch 500 cards per day. Not one could accomplish this because the goals had previously been set too low and employees became content. The next group of trainees were told that punching 750 cards per day was the norm, and to the surprise of management, they were able to reach that goal within a short period of time. For this reason Sanford made it a priority to re-enforce this regularly to his team.

Another method he used to get results from his staff was to explain the three types of feedback they could expect: positive, negative, or none—the one they should fear because it could mean extinction. They could expect to receive feedback in post-assignment debriefings like the military. Data would be reviewed against what was expected, what actually happened, and corrections needed to have a better outcome.

Sanford like to set goals with his team and re-enforced the word "team" often rather than focusing on the individual. His team had a list of low-stress goals, medium-stress goals, and high-stress goals. As they checked off all of the boxes of the low stress goals category, the medium goals became the low, and the high stress goals became the medium. Then there would be a new set of goals set for the high level. This worked very efficiently, and soon he had created a well-organized, efficient team capable of anything they set their mind to. Sam Harris, Teresa Dragar,

Zoey Luce, David Swayze, and Imran Watane were all very intelligent and capable analysts separately, but as a team they were a force of nature.

To complete their search for similar murders efficiently, each was taking a quadrant of the United States. They were entering criteria and then based on the results they would refine and narrow the search, each time reporting progress back to Sanford, who was updating his big whiteboard as they worked. The team was used to long hours and all had informed their families or significant others that today would be a long day and not to expect them home anytime soon.

Within twenty-four hours Sanford had two possible hits. The correlating criteria: was the cause of death: a fatal headshot; murder weapon was a .22 caliber magnum handgun; victim location was postmortem victim posed under tree; and the victim's body cleansed by undetermined means.

The mentality of this team was "define and refine," and they were rewarded early the next morning. The search had initially turned up a hit in Columbia, South Carolina, and another in Austin, Texas. The South Carolina murder took place in 1998, and the Texas unsolved case was from 2003. The murders occurred every five years—a consistent pattern.

The only sequence was defined by time. Why every five years? If it hadn't been for Detective Drozd finding the other murders, these two cold cases would probably never have been linked together. They would have stayed in the cold case files unsolved forever, but they were now out in the open.

This incredible work was what this FBI team thrived on. Information gathering and sorting took specific talents, and Sanford's team was the best. They got results, and Sanford was proud of their accomplishments.

Sanford decided it was time to give Drozd an early Christmas gift—new confirming evidence for his case which meant a better chance to solve it. He put together a data package and emailed him quickly, the subject line reading *Merry Christmas!*

Drozd's heart raced. He opened Sanford's email, scanning it. Agent Sanford was not misleading when he said Merry Christmas. The profile of a killer methodically killing and moving, killing and moving, was mostly complete. There was only one piece of the puzzle left to find.

Based on the results Sanford's team produced, there was only one hole left in the timeline—2008—but there was plenty of data to learn from the two crimes they had uncovered. Best of all, it confirmed all of his prior discoveries. There were plenty of crime scene pictures and information to read through. Sanford had already been pouring over the reports of each of these murders, and Drozd needed catch up.

Drozd responded to Sanford's email, asking if they could talk in six hours so he could update his murder board of facts and theories and become familiar with all of the new information. Sanford responded quickly with his cell number in case he was away from his desk.

CHAPTER FORTY

Y'all Can

1998
Columbia, South Carolina

Stacy Collins opened the door and entered the hallway. She walked up the steps and knocked on the door. The apartment was small but tastefully decorated. It was situated in a nice tenement in the affluent area of Columbia, South Carolina. Stacy was anxious to see Stephen. She was twenty-two, and a senior at the University of South Carolina, studying to become a physical therapist. She was well on her way to finishing her degree and looked forward to enter the job market within the next eighteen months. She was a blonde-haired, blue-eyed southern girl with an endearing accent. She was athletic and beautiful. By anyone's standards her confidence, intelligence, and charisma made her easy to be around.

She had no qualms about dating many guys. After all, she was young and figured it was the best time of her life, and she should thoroughly enjoy it. There were no shortage of suitors at college. She indulged, sampling a bevy of guys. Tonight was going to be no exception. A night off from studying was her reward. She would spend time with Stephen. She would enjoy his company and his lovemaking.

He was a wonderful, giving lover and knew how to pleasure her over and over again every time.

Stephen worked for a company specializing in advanced accounting software for large businesses. He enjoyed the challenge of selling to those that needed his product and those that didn't. He was twenty-eight years old and had the world in his hands with a good-paying job, a beautiful apartment, and he drove a newer model BMW. He had an appeal that was hard for women to resist, a sort of charm that disarmed people both in business and his personal life.

She knocked on the door and did not get an answer. It seemed strange, she had confirmed with him the week before, by leaving her usually flirty voicemail. But it wasn't an issue because she had a key which was kept in a small, zippered pocket at the bottom of her purse. Maybe he had to run an errand; there was never a set time she was expected. She unlocked and entered his apartment.

When she turned on the lights, there was a strange sight before her. All of the furniture and flooring were draped with sheets of plastic. Was Stephen having the place painted and that's why he was not around? She reached for her cell phone, the latest flip phone, a pink Motorola Razr, and before she knew it, a figure stepped out with a silenced pistol, raised it, and fired before she could even get her hands up. She dropped to the floor on top of the plastic sheets. The killer reflected for a moment, then methodically pulled the plastic sheet over her, brought out a washing machine-sized box which was hidden from plain site in the kitchen. It was beyond her field of sight when she entered the apartment. He carefully loaded her and all of the remaining sheets of plastic into the box, taking care not to touch anything, although he had rubber gloves with an extra layer of over-gloves on to protect leaving behind anything that might leave a trace of his being there. He wheeled the box to the stairs and carefully lowered it down one step at a time. No one noticed as he lifted the box onto the hydraulic ramp of a nondescript U-Haul truck of about twelve feet in length. It looked like a typical delivery. He drove off slowly down the street, careful to completely stop at signs and stay below the speed limit.

The next day Stacy's body was discovered in Harbinson State Forest next to a hiking trail. The sun had just come up and the resulting hues in the sky made it picturesque. The body sat peacefully under a tree with one dime-sized hole in her forehead.

She was found by a jogger who was out for her morning jog. The sun had come up at 6:58 that morning, which marked the opening of the park. The jogger was twenty minutes into her run when she found Stacy sitting peacefully. She turned and ran back to her car to get her phone and call for help, but Stacy was long dead and the killer was far away.

CHAPTER FORTY-ONE

Clean Getaway

Detectives had interviewed Stacy's friends and had a pretty good picture of her life. They discovered her proclivity for men in Columbia. They compiled a list of all of her lovers and diligently worked to bring each of them in for informal discussions. The detectives were looking for signs that someone knew more than they were letting on, but it was Stacy's girlfriend, Tanner, that provided the only solid clue to the events surrounding Stacy's murder. She told the detectives that Stacy had mentioned to her that she was going to see Stephen that evening to "blow off steam" after a wave of stressful tests. Tanner said that she understood that Stacy would not be home that evening. She also knew what Stacy meant when she used the phrase, "blow off steam" with Stephen, and it made her uncomfortable talking to the detectives about it. The detectives went to work tracking Stephen down and eventually were successful.

Stephen was questioned about Stacy's murder but was cleared when his alibi was confirmed by ten of his coworkers whom he was with at happy hour. That night happy hour lasted well into the night. Each of the corroborating witnesses placed him at the bar between the hours of 9:00 p.m. and 1:00 a.m. The autopsy confirmed the time of death was between 10:00 p.m. and 11:00 p.m. There was no chance he could be in two places at once unless he had taken lessons from Harry Houdini himself.

Detectives had brought him in for questioning prior to his claims of an alibi, and upon hearing of her death he was instantly visibly shaken by the news. The detectives had been very hard on him during the interrogation, trying to get him to slip up, but they found no signs of deception or inconsistency when they questioned him about why Stacy was at his apartment. He said they had a standing biweekly date, but he had forgotten about it and joined his coworkers at happy hour instead. He said she would also forget their dates from time to time which was no big deal because they had a friends-with-benefits arrangement. He continued to tell the detectives that by the time he realized he had made a mistake it was too late. He figured she would let herself into his apartment, realize he wasn't there, and then just leave. He didn't understand why she hadn't called. He was still shaky and clearly distraught over her death, but with the alibi confirmed the detectives had no reason to continue pursuing him as a suspect.

The case went cold, and because the detectives had nothing to go on, it became one of thousands of unsolved crimes.

CHAPTER FORTY-TWO

THE GHOST

The six hours had passed, and it was late afternoon when Detective Drozd called Agent Sanford. The call went to voicemail, so he tried the cell number Sanford had provided. Sanford picked up on the second ring with a humorous greeting, "Santa Claus here, can I help you? You must have been a good boy to get such a present this year." Drozd joined in laughing and said playfully, "I've been a very good boy this year, Santa. It was a giant help," said Drozd, stating the obvious. "I have been through everything on the South Carolina case but haven't gotten through the Texas one yet. There was a lot of information in your analysis. My whiteboard is starting to look like a roadmap. I'll need a little bit more time on the Texas case, but I'm pretty up to speed on Stacy from Columbia, so let's start there."

Sanford was animated, saying, "This guy is a freakin' ghost! I reached out to both offices individually but got the same exact response: a big, fat, nothing! Neither had any more information to share. They did a lot of legwork and beat on quite a few doors, but no slipups from this ghost. There's nothing, not a hair, print, footprint, or anything that would let you know he was ever there. I thought about flying out to those places, but then I realized those crimes occurred so long ago that the odds of finding anything useful were none. So I did the next best thing and spoke with the law enforcement offices that handled the cases. I even reached out to the FBI offices in that area. Nobody had a shred of evidence nor motive, means, or opportunity."

Drozd liked this guy more and more because they spoke the same language. He also knew they were going to have to find some common ground between the cases to start to explain motive.

Sanford continued, "Well, no matter where we start, they both say exactly the same thing: they found nothing. No trace evidence, no real motive, no likely suspects because everyone close to the victims had confirmed alibis. There were indiscretions, but nothing ever came of either of their investigations."

Drozd was perplexed by the various locations of the crimes and asked, "We need to understand why this guy is moving around! Is it a job? Is he a transient? Once we get a handle on that, we need to understand how he's choosing his victims? Do the 'indiscretions' have anything to do with it? Does that match up with the three murders that I have here?" He stood up from his chair then put the pen in his fingers and started the dexterous exercise of moving it between them quickly. "I'm getting a bit fired up," he exclaimed. "My head is spinning from all these 'what ifs' right now! Tell me what you meant by indiscretions."

"Since you've looked at the Collins case, let's start with South Carolina. Stacy was a student at the University of South Carolina. She was a senior, doing well, and seemed to have her act together, based on what the detectives gathered from the interviews of her circle of friends, teachers, and the men she dated. The consensus was she may have been promiscuous, but there is nothing criminal about that.

Some people just aren't built for monogamy, and she was one."

Drozd was writing on notecards quickly because some of this incidental information was based on conclusions of the original investigators from conversations with those who knew the victims, but because it was a mix of impressions and intuition, wasn't included in the formal reports Sanford had provided. But that word, "monogamy," stuck out to Drozd. He couldn't put his finger on it, not quite yet, but knew he would soon. For now, it was just out of reach.

Drozd asked, "Did they track down all of her love interests?"

"As far as they could determine, they were all accounted for and interviewed. They had one good suspect who was a 'friend-with-benefits' gentleman named Stephen. He was confirmed to have had a scheduled, biweekly rendezvous with Stacy. It was supposed to take place the evening she was killed, but conveniently, he forgot about it. The only thing that saved him and kept the detectives from digging deeper into him was the fact that he had an iron-clad alibi with ten witnesses. Game over."

"Let's discuss what my murder board says as of right now." He had gotten up and stood in front of his whiteboard with a dry erase pen in hand. He was pointing at it as they went through it one line at a time. "The timeline is interesting and almost complete. Here is what I have as of right now. In 1988, Danny Johnson was murdered, labeled 'a drug deal gone bad.' Maybe that wasn't the real reason, but I'm still working that one. In 1993, ski bum Elliot Kidd may have had an indiscretion because his girlfriend had to call looking for him for anyone to even realize he was missing.

And lastly, we have my 2013 victim, Shelly Lynn, who was definitely having relations with a mystery someone."

Sanford said, "Sounds like infidelity might be the common link. At least it's a start. Well, I have the information on the Texas victim, but it sounds like you need a bit more time to fill in all the blanks on that one ,so why don't we reconvene tomorrow morning, say 9:00? We can speak about him and the timeline."

Drozd agreed and after disconnecting, went back to work, but only after he brewed a new pot of coffee. It was going to be a long night.

The chessboard was full of pieces and the moves were becoming clearer by the minute. He and Agent Sanford needed to play the game cleanly, thinking their moves through thoroughly before taking their finger off the piece, to have a chance to win the game.

CHAPTER FORTY-THREE

Exes Live In Texas

2003
Austin, Texas

Most cities in Texas are overrun with cement overpasses and endless highways, but Austin has a different feel to it. That's why Thad Sokol was happy he got the job at the University of Texas. He had moved here to take the job of head coach of the women's volleyball team. This was a step up from his previous jobs as an assistant coach.

He had worked hard to learn from all the head coach mentors he had in his past positions. Now he was ready to be the person in charge, to see what he could build and create with this team. This was a new chapter for him and his wife, a new city, a new job, and the potential to improve his status in the coaching world.

He was tall, a little over 6' 3". He had black hair and blue eyes. He was of Russian descent on his father's side and South African on his mother's. He got his height from his grandfather, who was well north of 6' tall. His height was a benefit when he played competitive volleyball during college. He was an outside hitter or wing spiker, as some referred to it. He loved the competition and had been part of teams that won numerous national honors and titles.

When his competitive career ended, he just couldn't get it out of his blood, so after graduating he got experience as a volunteer assistant coach. Then he got promoted to a paid assistant coaching position the next year, and four years later he moved to a better college program as an assistant coach where he stayed for eight years. And now, finally, at 35-years old, he got his big chance as the head coach of a pretty decent women's volleyball program. He was hoping, with good recruiting this year, the following year could be even better, maybe even a shot at a national title.

Thad, and his wife, Diana, had been married for twelve years. She was a very nice person, the quintessential "girl next door." She might not turn heads at the bar, but she was a solid person of even temperament. She wasn't overweight nor underweight. She was cute, but not considered beautiful. She wasn't well educated, so she was not overly concerned with her own career. She was content to change jobs whenever Thad had needed to move to further his career.

She had suffered through some hard times with Thad because of his temper. She felt this new chapter in their lives would be good for their relationship, a new start. They had been here seven months, and she felt things were going well.

Thad arrived three months before her to start the job while she tied up the loose ends at their home in Arizona. She had to sell the house, which took a little bit longer than she would have liked, but the time passed quickly, and she actually enjoyed the time on her own, maybe a bit too much, she thought.

It was mid-October and the women's volleyball team had just suffered a heartbreaking loss to Missouri, who was ranked just ahead of Texas in the preseason Big 12 Coaches

Poll. Thad was really upset with the team, the officials, and the world in general at that moment. He wanted that win. He needed that win.

After the debriefing with the team directly after the match ended, he went to his office and added notes to his "2003 Season" spreadsheet. He documented the game plan, what actually happened during the game, and what the team needed to work on to improve for the next game. He had learned this process of debriefing from reading many books about military procedures. He felt it was a good model to help the team learn from their mistakes, adapt, and overcome.

He checked his text messages and saw one that read "new car." The rest of the text simply stated "512-555-1212, come for test drive." He knew what this meant and thought to himself, I deserve this. I work hard.

He called Diana and told her that he needed to stay late and review game film while everything was still fresh in his mind. She said it wasn't a problem and that she was turning in early because she had to be at work by 9:00 the next morning. She asked him to please be quiet when he came home so she could be well rested. He said, "No problem, I'll see you soon."

He called the number from the text message and nobody answered. He was upset but within thirty seconds a text appeared with an address and message stating, "See you soon, door will be unlocked." He made note of the address and then deleted the text, always trying to be careful. He packed up his laptop and headed out the door.

He drove the eighteen minutes to the location, feeling excited in anticipation of what was about to happen. He had started visiting services like this more often when they became easier to find on the internet. He pulled up in front of the apartment, which was one of twenty in the building. This one was on the first floor. This was just like any apartment complex with rows and rows of buildings designed for affordable housing, nothing special.

He walked up to the door and lightly knocked and then tried the knob. It opened just as the text had promised. There was a faint voice from another room that said, "Please take off your shoes and leave them by the front door." This was customary with Asian households. After a pause, the faint voice said, "I'm in here, please come in."

Thad's pulse raced, and he shook a bit with anticipation, like he was shivering. He entered the room, which was only lit with a dim red light, the sheets of the bed slightly drawn.

From the bathroom a faint voice said, "Please get comfortable."

Thad sat on the edge of the bed. He always wanted to make sure the woman was "as promised" before he got too comfortable. His head was lowered until the door to the bathroom slowly opened, and before he knew it, a man wearing a black face mask stepped out quickly, raised a gun, and in a split second, pulled the trigger. No noise, just the spit of a silenced gun. Thad never had a chance to think, react, or anything. It probably was like someone just turned off the light switch, everything going dark and silent instantly. But this was for forever, not just until someone turned the light switch back on.

The killer worked quickly and efficiently. He was becoming better and better at this process. He knew exactly what needed to be done. After the kill, he knew the best time to move the body and how to move it without even a hint of suspicion. He already knew where he was going to deposit this body, so he simply ran down his mental checklist and accomplished each step one at a time.

The next morning it was a balmy sixty-three degrees by 7:15. The first people to climb to the Pennybacker Bridge overlook found Thad. He was resting against a tree, looking like he had just sat down to take a long look at the scenic view. The only thing out of the ordinary was a small dime-shaped hole in his forehead.

By the time the report came in and the crime scene officers had located his wallet and an identification card, Diana was already at work. She hadn't given his absence a second thought that morning because occasionally Thad would sleep at the office. He was dedicated to succeeding.

The officers had found his university ID and contacted the main office. They referred the officers to the appropriate people to help locate his next of kin. After some due diligence, they found Diana's place of work, drove there, and sadly broke the news of Thad's death to her. She broke down and had to be taken to the hospital and sedated.

There was no evidence, no witnesses, no motive. Just a lifeless body. The killer was long gone.

CHAPTER FORTY-FOUR

COACH SOKOL

Detective Drozd had only gone home last evening for a short time to sleep, shower, and change clothes. He had fallen asleep as soon as his head hit the pillow. He was exhausted, his body was in need of the phase of sleep known as REM or Rapid Eye Movement. It is the phase of sleep right before a person falls into a deep sleep cycle. REM sleep helps the mind let go of the stresses of the day. But tonight, Drozd simply passed out and slept with no dreams at all. He awoke at six in the morning after a solid four-and-a-half hours of sleep. He showered, did ten minutes of push-ups and sit-ups to get his blood flowing, and then got dressed and ran out the door, coffee in hand. At 7:00 a.m. Drozd arrived back at his office. He was already on his second cup of coffee as he had finished the first on the drive in.

He was fresh and ready for the day. He still had a bit of time before his call with FBI Agent Sanford so he decided to run through his board one more time. He noted all the progress they had made in the last 48 hours. It was amazing and exciting! This is what he preferred to be doing, rather than picking up pieces of drug dealer and gang banger murders. This was exhilarating, and he thrived on it. He knew that if he were successful in solving and closing these cases, there would have to be changes in his life. He wasn't sure if he could go back to the mundane routine of working the typical Mon Valley crimes again. He drifted for a second, wondering what might be next for his career. Then he snapped back to reality. It was time to make a move on his chess board. The killer technically had never made a bad move in the game; nonetheless, Drozd still felt he was starting to make progress to catch up in this match.

He noted the big empty space in the timeline: the five-year pattern had appeared slowly during the investigation. But what happened in 2008? This was the big question to be answered. Between Sanford's team and his own research, they had turned over every stone they could find. They had mined a lot of gold in this expedition. He paused on this for a few seconds. He still couldn't figure out what they had missed. Did the killer change his ritual for that murder or did something happen in 2008 that didn't allow him to follow his pattern? He had returned to the cycle in 2013, back on track. Drozd thought this guy wouldn't break the pattern, he's way too methodical. He didn't know the answer to this question.

Then he thought of something strange. He started thinking of therapist Charlotte Burnett. She had flirted with him. He flirted back. They shared a moment. He liked it. She was smart and seemed nice. His curiosity was piqued. He decided he wanted to get to know her better. Furthermore, he wanted her help with the case. Maybe she could provide input on the psyche of the killer. First he would ask for Sanford's blessing because they were now partners. Charlotte Burnett deserved to help find the answers. After all, she had gone out on a moral limb by providing information about her patient, Shelly Lynn. He was glad she had shared. It was one of the first breadcrumbs of information that helped his investigation. If he got

Sanford's blessing he would call Charlotte—for more than one reason, he chuckled to himself.

At 9:00 a.m., Drozd called Sanford's office phone. After exchanging pleasantries, they got down to business. Drozd asked, "What do you know that I don't about Thad Sokol? I see reports that say a whole lot of nothing, except for the fact that he is dead and was murdered in the same method as our other victims."

Sanford said, "Well, I do have some extra information that we came by through some different channels. Thad Sokol's phone account revealed he was a customer of an Asian prostitution ring. This associates him with less than upstanding citizens, but they probably weren't serial killers who gently clean and place their victims' bodies. Human trafficking falls into the organized crime category in my opinion. I think it's safe to say this falls into our category of indiscretions,' wouldn't you?"

"That does fit pretty well."

Answering him Sanford said emphatically, "Yep."

Drozd thought they may have found a common thread that linked all the victims. Drozd then turned a bit more professional in his tone saying, "Carlos, I want to bring in Shelly Lynn's therapist on this indiscretion' theory. Her name is Charlotte Burnett. She seems like a good person and helped me when she didn't have to. I think her input might give us some new perspective. Would you be okay with that?"

Sanford was quiet for a moment, obviously thinking it through. "I don't have a problem with that as long as you tread softly. A lot of these'theories' are just that for now."

Drozd had the answer he wanted. It opened a couple of different paths he could follow with Burnett.

Drozd updated his murder board with Sanford's new Asian prostitution information using a dry erase marker to write under the picture of Thad Sokol. After linking the pictures with connecting lines, he wrote the word, "indiscretion." But there was a flaw with this theory—Danny Johnson. He was only known to have been involved in a drug deal gone wrong. Was there more to it than that? His mind was racing to process this question.

Drozd brought it up to Sanford, saying "There's one flaw in our indiscretion theory. Danny Johnson's murder was a drug deal gone bad, unless we missed something on that one." Drozd was walking in circles while talking.

Sanford said, "Settle down and take a second." He could hear the stress in Drozd's voice. "Take a moment to review your data, recheck it, and then if we need to adjust our theory, let's jump off that bridge when we come to it," Sanford said even-toned. "I personally believe there is more to the Danny Johnson story than we have been made aware of. Maybe that's where you should concentrate your efforts in the short term." Sanford's strength was managing and coordinating a team, even giving Drozd direction now.

Drozd said, "Okay, you're right. Let's shift to the other elephant in the room."

"That being?" asked Sanford.

"The timeline," stated Drozd emphatically.

"What do you think about the lack of an incident in 2008? asked Drozd. He continued his train of thought saying, "We've checked under every rock possible. Where do we go from here?"

Sanford said, "My team and I have been working this, and we may have come up with more information. First, we rechecked everything, concentrating our efforts on 2008 around the country. Nothing new turned up, so the team started to think outside the box and decided to look outside the United States. Right now they are checking all the international records they can access. If it's out there they'll find it."

Drozd went from frazzled to dazzled, and stated, "I didn't even think of that. Wouldn't that be something if our ghost went international?" Drozd continued, "Your team is going to have to take point on that search since it's way out of my league." The energy between Drozd and Sanford was contagious. They were both in their element.

Sanford replied, "We're on it. You work on the timeline and Danny Johnson while we do our thing over here, okay?"

Drozd could hardly contain himself but said, "Call when you find anything, no matter what time of the day or night it is." With that they disconnected.

It was still early enough that Drozd might be able to work on his assignment. He would contact and visit Gerry Mae Johnson to see if she knew of any "indiscretions" that Danny might have been involved in. He dialed her number and waited for her to pick up the phone.

CHAPTER FORTY-FIVE

THE POND CLEARS

Gerry Mae Johnson picked up the phone on the fourth ring, answering, "Hello."

Drozd politely identified himself saying, "Hello, Ms. Johnson, this is Detective Drozd from the Monessen Police Department. Have I called at a convenient time?"

She spoke in a frail voice, saying, "Yes, Detective, I'm just doing a few chores around the house after eating a little lunch. What can I do for you?"

He asked if he could come and visit her and ask her a few more questions.

She said, "Yes, I can do that. How about three o'clock?"

He confirmed, saying, "Perfect."

He made the short trip across the river in a reasonable amount of time and arrived at 2:55 p.m. He didn't need to check his notes for the correct apartment. He walked up to the door and knocked lightly. Gerry Mae answered as quickly as she could make her way to the door. She offered him some water, and he politely accepted.

Drozd interlocked his fingers and asked her how she had been. She replied that she was the same as always with good days and bad days. Then she asked him if he had any new information about her son's case.

He said, "Ms. Johnson, we have been following up on all leads. But we really could use a little more help from you. We just need a bit more information, if you can provide it. Can you tell me if Danny ever had any problems in a relationship with a girl?"

Ms. Johnson slowly tilted her head up and looked at the ceiling like she saw someone that wasn't there. She replied, "Danny was no saint because of what he did to earn his money. He had girls throwing themselves at him for one reason or another all the time. So I really can't narrow it down for you to just one. The only one I ever raised hell with him about was this little girl from Donora." She searched for the name and then her eyes lit up as it came to her, "Terri something or other. I was furious because she was underage, and he was already in trouble with the law. I asked him, "Why give them more things to harass you with?" All the other ones were probably just looking to score some drugs so I guess there probably would be a lot of problems with women…"

Drozd's eyes shot open after she said the name *Terri*! Before she had even finished the rest of the sentence, he stammered out the name, "Terri Lynn?" He almost cut her off in mid-sentence.

She looked up at him quickly, gaining direct eye contact. She replied back quickly, "Does that name mean something?"

Drozd composed himself and said, "It may, but I'm going to have to follow up on a few things before I can definitively know anything. It may be nothing at all, but, it might be something."

Ms. Johnson said, "What is it about that girl and my son? Do you think she had something to do with his murder?" She was about as agitated as she had been in quite a long time.

Drozd downplayed the information. But the top of his head was about to pop off as his mind raced. He replied, "I am not sure of anything yet, Ms. Johnson. Like I said, I'll need to follow up on a few things before I'll know its significance. It could be nothing at all, and I don't want to get your hopes up. But know I appreciate everything that you have told ,me and I take it very seriously. I will follow up and return to share anything I learn." He stood up and extended his hand. He thanked her for the water and the conversation and headed for the door.

He exited the building at a normal pace but then started walking faster to get back into his car as quickly as possible and get back to the office. He had calls to make. His brain was running the angles: Terri Lynn, indiscretion, murders. This new information about Shelly's mom, Terri, revealed more moves that could be made. He needed to get in touch with therapist Charlotte Burnett. Maybe she could tie some of the facts together. Second on his list was reporting back to Sanford. Sanford was right, there was more to Danny Johnson than they originally thought. Everything was coming together, and his heart was racing.

He dialed Charlotte. She answered on the third ring, and started flirting right away. "Detective Drozd I presume?" She continued "If you keep calling so often people are going to start to talk about us."

He played right along saying, "Your on-time phone caller here, ma'am. Let them talk, it's good for my image to be associated with a successful, beautiful woman."

They both laughed then quickly started acting professionally. But there was no turning back now, the tone had been set. They were going to have their own chess match.

Drozd was in front of his murder board, standing, and spinning a pen from one finger to another. It went faster and faster until he finally dropped it. He bent down and picked it up.

Their conversation centered on his "indiscretions theory" as being the motive for the murders. He asked her opinion of how she thought it tied them all together.

She stated, "It sounds like a solid assumption, and maybe it was the lynchpin between the victims."

At the same time, she had questions like he did. *Why were the murders all over the nation? Why every five years? What happened in 2008? Why clean and pose the bodies?*

She started profiling the murderer psyche a bit for him. "If infidelity was the motive for the murders, how would he know how to choose his victims? Did they cheat on him and that is why he did what he did? That theory has a major flaw to it because the victims have been male and female."

The pond, that was clear now, muddied again. Two steps forward one step back, he thought.

There were still so many questions to be answered and things were moving fast. He told her he would touch base as soon as he had more to tell her, but before he disconnected, he said, "What celebrity do you think you look like?"

She giggled, paused for a moment, and said, "People tell me I look like Demi Moore," and with that she hung up, leaving him wanting more.

He thought, *I love Demi Moore.*

CHAPTER FORTY-SIX

INTERNATIONAL FLAVOR

Detective Drozd steadied his thoughts and tried to regain his composure after that final teasing remark from Charlotte Burnett, claiming to resemble Demi Moore. He needed to put that out of his mind. This was going to be a very tough task now with that image burned into his brain. With a great amount of will and discipline, he forced himself to compartmentalize things for now.

He had new information about Danny Johnson that needed to be shared with Agent Sanford. He felt their chances of catching this killer were drastically improved by removing the question of what was the actual motive for Johnson's murder. Drozd's suspicions that Gavin Dean wasn't Shelly's killer were now solidified with the new information he possessed. There was a murderer out there, hunting and killing. Not even killing, he was executing people. There were still many questions to be answered to find the murderer. He had just taken a big step toward this by taking Dean off the murder board. That narrowed down the search and would allow him to focus on finding the real killer.

Drozd felt completely alive. He was exactly where he wanted to be, doing exactly what he wanted to do. And maybe even one step closer to being with someone he wanted to be with. A person is capable of great things when they are in this state of mind. But it was time to get back to reality, he thought.

He called Sanford's cellphone. It was past business hours at FBI headquarters, but Drozd was anxious to update him with his progress on his assignment.

Sanford greeted him pleasantly saying, "Hello there, my friend."

Drozd, relaxed his tone, sensing that Sanford had some news, and said, "Hello right back at you. It's been a good day over here," he stated.

Sanford said. "Been a good day over here also."

Drozd's curiosity was piqued.

Sanford continued, "You go first. We'll consider this a game of 'show and tell,' then we'll follow it up with a game of twenty questions on the back end. There will be a prize to the one who had the better day," he said in jest.

Drozd was in his usual area in his office. It was a big office, not fancy, but built for efficiency. He was a very organized person, and it showed in the appearance of his space. There were no stacks of papers cluttering the top of his desk. There was no trash overflowing the garbage bin which sat underneath it. His whiteboard was neat and organized, with the dry erase markers lined up and color coded and ready for use. He had room to move around, not only by walking, but sometimes free-wheeling on his chair, back and forth to whatever area he needed to be in at that particular time. He was comfortable and productive here in his office.

Drozd began the conversation, "Okay, to start with, you were right regarding Danny Johnson. I think he might be the killer's first crime. Johnson's mom told me her son had an affair with none other than Terri Lynn, Shelly's mom, while she was underage. This was back in the 1980s, when the murders started. The mom wasn't exactly sure of the dates. She said there were many girls that came and went because he dealt drugs. She said the affair with Terri had been the only one that caused her personal grief, because if Danny got caught with an underage girl the police would make sure he paid for it dearly and would likely be jailed. She said this is why Terri stuck out in her mind, because of this fear."

Sanford responded, "Well, that's definitely an indiscretion! It also aligns with our theory. Great work!"

Drozd's voice dropped a bit saying, "But there are still so many questions to be answered. The sheer number of them is mind boggling."

With an authoritarian voice, Sanford said, "Man, take the win. Doesn't matter how big or small it is, a win is a win. Do you realize that the questions that are weighing on your mind are being answered one at a time? It takes time to solve something this complex. It's a process, but together we can get it done!" Sanford's strength shone through again. He knew how to keep his people positive and motivated, making them understand the task at hand. Sanford made a statement that definitely raised Drozd eyebrows and spirits saying, "I'm about to make your day!"

Sanford started to explain, "My team did their job. They have been searching all databases worldwide focusing on our cause of death in 2008. Here's what they turned up: They found the needle in the haystack in San Jose, Costa Rica. A young woman, thought to be an escort, was found in a small park sitting under a tree with a small bullet hole in her forehead. Sound familiar?" Sanford hit send on his computer and sent Drozd the files that he had on this international unsolved murder.

Drozd exclaimed, "Unreal! I'm just getting the files now." He clicked on the folder and started browsing through them. He said, "I can't believe your team! This completes the killer's cycle and our timeline! Did the authorities ever arrest anyone?" Drozd quickly corrected himself saying, "That was a dumb question. I guess it was rhetorical."

Sanford replied, "Our ghost doesn't leave any footprints, literally."

They continued on with the "twenty questions" portion of the game but at the end agreed that no clear winner could be declared in the "better day" game. They decided to sleep on their new information and start the next day with their minds uncluttered after a good night's rest. They also agreed to savor a good day because indeed it was!

The chess board had many pieces left on it and there were many ways the game could turn if his team made any mistakes. They were right in the heart of the game and Drozd was excited for the battle to come!

CHAPTER FORTY-SEVEN

HOTEL CALIFORNIA

2008
San Jose, Costa Rica

The Hotel Del Ray was an infamous landmark in San Jose, Costa Rica. Its huge exterior was painted pink, making it hard, if not impossible, to miss. The hotel was built by three partners, two from the United States and one from England. It was mostly known for the beautiful women working there, who were quite willing to provide the gentlemen a very nice time for a decent price.

The hotel had a full casino, dance club, and restaurant that complimented the three different bars. The clientele consisted of many expatriates who came for the beautiful women of Costa Rica, Columbia, and other neighboring countries. The beautiful women needed to support their families. There was no stigma in this industry among the people of Costa Rica. They had a positive attitude, and the government only slightly regulated the oldest trade in the world.

Bobby Reynolds was lonely. It had been a long time since he had been lucky enough to be with a woman, let alone one of the beautiful women that worked at Del Ray. He had learned of the hotel when a pop up link appeared while he was browsing online two months ago. He had done a little research and decided it was worth a try. He renewed his passport, bought the plane ticket, and made his hotel reservation. The hotel provided a shuttle to and from the airport. The bellman greeted him and took his bag while he checked in.

The clerk checked him in and gave the bellman the key to his room. Bobby was in 516. There were six floors in the Hotel Del Ray, and it was rumored that one of the owners lived on the sixth floor, full time. The first thing to catch Bobby's eye was the door of his room. It featured a carved iguana sitting on a branch under the leaves of a palm tree. Each door in the hotel had a different carving. The bellman, Oscar, opened the door and took the bag inside, placing Bobby's bag on a shelf just beyond the entrance to the bathroom. The king-sized bed was to the left and there was a chair in the opposite corner. An air conditioner cooled the room to a pleasant 70 degrees. A large towel folded in the shape of a swan was in the center of the bed. The room was not amazing, but it certainly would do.

Oscar said, "Mr. Reynolds, during the day, the ladies may negotiate for a better rate, but in the evening their rate is pretty standard. There will be many beautiful ladies this weekend at our hotel. Please be careful and put all your valuables, including your passport, in the safe which is located right here," he pointed to it sitting on a shelf. Oscar explained how to secure the safe and asked, "Do you have any other needs that I may assist with?" Bobby shook his head and tipped him ten dollars which was a nice tip. The bellman thanked him and went on his way.

It was three o'clock in the afternoon which was really five o'clock to Bobby, taking into account the time change between the United States and Costa Rica. He was tired from the trip, so he decided to lie down for a short rest before cleaning up and visiting the bar. He thought he might get a bite to eat before the evening started. He lay down and drifted off, quickly awaking at 6:15 p.m. After showering and dressing, he ventured down the stairs which were located right outside his door. He thought a little exercise couldn't hurt to get his blood flowing. He was positive that going down the stairs would be much easier than climbing back up five flights. Back on the first level, he could see the bars were just starting to come to life, along with the casino located between the three bars. He went across the street and into the restaurant for dinner. His beef with fries was good. He ordered bottled water and remembered to not use ice. He had read about avoiding intestinal problems in South America on the internet. He had a cup of coffee which was grown in Costa Rica, and it was the best he had ever tasted. It was smooth and nutty. He thought he could definitely get used to this. After he finished, he paid the bill and ambled back across the road to the hotel and into the bar.

He sat at a small table and ordered a rum and Coke. There were sports on all of the televisions. Unfortunately, the broadcasts were in Spanish so he would have to settle for the visual. The waitress returned a few minutes later, setting the drink down and collecting payment. He realized he wasn't there to watch sports but for something else. He shifted his focus to all of the extremely beautiful women who were mingling with the male patrons. They were young and beautiful, with age and genetics on their side. Their beauty was unmatched in most places in the world. They were from different parts of South America and were tall and thin with beautiful complexions. Many spoke only very limited English, but that usually didn't matter. After the man had asked for a date, they would take him by the hand

and lead him to the elevator. That man knew this small period of time he got to spend with one of these beautiful creatures would be one of the best moments of his life.

Bobby saw her sitting at the bar. She was talking to another woman who sat to her left. From the back he thought she was beautiful but when she finally got up and turned around and he saw her face, his heart beat faster. He was sure this was the beauty he wanted to spend time with, but he was nervous. She spotted him as her head swiveled side to side, her eyes searching the bar. There he was, just as she had been told. She knew about him, his description, and the fact that he had money. She had received a message from a former client/friend that this particular gentleman would be at the hotel this weekend. He asked that she make sure he had a very nice time. He also informed her that he would send extra money so she was more than enthusiastic to make an extra effort. The only stipulation was she wasn't to mention anything about him. He wanted to remain anonymous but make sure his friend enjoyed the weekend. He told her that he trusted no one else with this job. She smiled and thought for a moment about years ago when she had the opportunity to spend her life with her former client/friend. What would it have been like? She pushed the thought out of her mind and went to work.

She got up and approached Bobby and within five minutes they were speaking, her with broken English, about everything and nothing for almost two-and-a-half hours. They shared drinks and laughed. Finally, she took his hand and said, "Let's go, mi amor." Without hesitation they took the elevator up to his room.

This was the luckiest moment of his life, to be remembered forever.

CHAPTER FORTY-EIGHT

TIME OF YOUR LIFE

The elevator climbed the five floors slower than Bobby Reynolds could have imagined. But he took the time to admire Angelica. They held hands and he even snuck a small kiss from the softest lips he had ever encountered. Finally, the elevator stopped, and they exited, weaving their way through the hallways until they arrived at the door of his room.

Once inside, Angelica asked, "May I use your restroom?"

Bobby answered, "Of course."

She slipped into the bathroom and closed the door, and Bobby heard the shower come to life. He thought the shower was so lucky to have that beautiful woman in it. Five minutes later, Angelica exited the bathroom with nothing covering her perfectly-shaped body. She was about 5'6" without her heels. She had a thin waist, long legs and the face of an angel, all complemented by big brown eyes. Her blonde hair fell just below her shoulders and had brown highlights. She was perfection. He couldn't believe his fortune to get the opportunity to make love to this beautiful creature.

Angelica asked, "Do you like?" She was just wearing a smile. He thought if ever there was a rhetorical question, this was it. She was perfect.

She was twenty-four years old, had amazing skin tone, zero percent body fat, and enhanced breasts that were proportionate to her body. She had a smile that made him feel like there was no better place to be in the entire world. He gestured for her to come to him and she made her way across the room. They embraced and enjoyed a long sensual kiss.

They made love for about 30 minutes and then lay there with elevated heart rates, basking in the most pleasurable experience two humans can have. He felt alive in the moment, his brain swirling with endorphins. After about ten minutes it was time for her to shower and leave. He didn't want it to end She took another shower and a few minutes later exited the restroom, fully dressed and ready to return to the bar downstairs. He dressed, escorted her back to the elevator, and it took them back downstairs. They kissed lightly right before they arrived at the lobby. He was very sad to see their time end.

Later that evening he was sitting in the lobby of the hotel when he saw Angelica again, this time with another man, walking arm and arm. He felt sadness and anger. He was an emotional basket case. There was nothing he could do or say so he just sat. That was the last time he saw her.

Angelica left the Hotel Del Ray at around eleven o'clock. She decided she would move on to one more location to ply her trade. When she left, she walked south two blocks, and a man walked up behind her.

He summoned her, gesturing for her to wait, then asked her, "Haven't we met at the Del Ray?" She answered,

"It's possible." He then asked in a disarmingly pleasant tone if she was free.

She said, "I'm available," and agreed to the date. He looked familiar, but she couldn't quite place him. This was not uncommon because she met a lot of people.

He told her they could walk back to his hotel but when he mentioned that he only wanted to be orally pleasured, she thought this was an opportunity for a quick turn-around. Instead, she suggested that they have their date in the alley just off to the left of where they were standing. They moved deep into the shadows, and she dropped to her knees, reaching for the zipper on his pants. She never saw it coming. He reached behind his back and brought the gun around, raising the pistol up in one smooth, fast motion. He executed her as she started to look up. She probably didn't even register what was happening.

The next morning they found Angelica's body in a small park by a tree a few blocks from the hotel. There was a small bullet hole in her forehead, but strangely enough there was no blood. It was as if the wound had been cleaned. She looked very peaceful.

The police did make some inquiries at the hotel since it was known she frequented the establishment. The inquiries were fruitless because it was impossible to know everyone she had spent time with. Her murder led to changes in the hotel's policy—all guests had to register the ladies they spent time with so there would be records.

The police had nothing to really base an investigation on, so they gave up after a short period of time. They reasoned it could have just been a robbery gone bad. They never solved the case. The killer was long gone.

CHAPTER FORTY-NINE

CLOSING IN

The next morning Drozd awoke fresh and ready. The night before he had trouble falling asleep as his mind was very active with thoughts of the past ten days and what was to come. He dreamed of being chased or maybe he was chasing something. He just hoped he didn't wake up tired from all the running, he chuckled to himself. But when deep sleep did take over, he got the restorative amount he needed to perform optimally the next day.

He followed his normal routine, starting with a light breakfast of eggs, cereal, and fresh berries. No breakfast would be complete without his coffee. He savored the first swallow as it warmed his throat and insides.

He allowed himself to think of Charlotte for a few minutes. What would it be like to know her? Would they have chemistry? He knew they had a good vibe and playful conversation. He also respected her for her professional abilities and empathy toward her patients. And, yes, he had that damn image of her from her playful description of herself. Was she really that attractive? The looks of Demi Moore and intelligence. That would be an amazing combination!

He got in his car and drove to the office. His murder whiteboard was up to date with the new timeline. The unsolved murder in 2008 in Costa Rica was now in place. Gavin Dean had been removed as a suspect. He was another victim as Drozd saw it. The murder motive for Danny Johnson now read "indiscretion" like the others on the board. Things had lined up. But now how would the team tie everything together?

Drozd called Agent Sanford. He was standing today, not sitting down because he wanted to stay alert and be able to reference and update the board quickly if need be. Sanford answered immediately, asking, "Are we fresh and ready to go today, Detective Drozd?"

Drozd shot back, "Locked, loaded and ready to roll, Agent Sanford," he said firmly.

Sanford responded, "Good, let's figure out how to catch our ghost today."

They discussed the steps needed to narrow down the search. They now had something that left a trail, due to this being an international murder. There would be a record of the killer entering and leaving Costa Rica. Passport Control records could provide that information. That was one thing that all countries of the world had in common, they wanted to know who was coming and who was going. The team hoped it might be the one mistake the killer had made.

Sanford said, "I'm going to have to play by the rules on this one. Those records are hard to get and require cutting through a lot of red tape. Sometimes Costa Rica likes us and sometimes they are a bit salty. Let's hope they are in a generous mood today," he concluded.

So that's where you are going to put all your efforts today? I think that's the wise choice, but I'm afraid I will be of no help to you on this one."

"No need. The team will be on this. I want you to review your board and look closely. Find something small, something that might seem like nothing but may turn out to be big. Sometimes it's the small things that help us turn the corner in a case. Just keep working it, Detective."

They disconnected without scheduling another meeting. Each knew the other would reach out as things developed. The investigation was becoming more fluid.

Drozd sat in his chair and started throwing a rubber ball against the wall of his office and catching it. This was one of his relaxation techniques. The wall provided the perfect rebound, each time bringing the ball back in his general direction. He had just caught it when he heard the familiar ding on his computer as a new email was delivered.

He rolled his chair in front of his desk, clicked on the email, and started to read.

From: info@LetsDoThis.com Subject Line: Client Access

The email stated: *We are currently in conversations with our legal team in regards to our responsibility to the privacy of our patrons. We are taking under consideration that this is a murder investigation and will try to provide an answer in a timely manner. Thank you, Pascal, site manager.*

Drozd was not upset. It was exactly what he had expected from this type of website. They would certainly be covering their butts. Setting his ball on the top of his desk, he typed a return email. The subject line read: *Time is of the essence.* In the body of the email he begged for a quick answer. He stated, *the killer may get away if there were any big delays.*

Drozd wasn't that upset because, in the big picture, they were in a good position. He thought if they could get the passport information to narrow suspects down, it would tilt the chessboard in their favor.

Two hours later he was on his third cup of coffee and starting to become a little bit wired. The caffeine was working its magic. He happened to look at his murder board and something caught his eye. It was hanging in a small bag in the corner of the board. A small pin that read C-U-P, which stood for California University of Pennsylvania. A bolt of lightning struck, and he nearly jumped out of his chair. He quickly moved to the board and grabbed the bag and examined the insignia on it. There it was, the small thing that Sanford had asked for, the school connection to Shelly Lynn. In a prior conversation, this connection was confirmed by the therapist. It was the other man, the black silhouette with the question mark. He was right here all along, so close to them. California University of Pennsylvania was located less than twenty minutes from Drozd's office.

Coursing with adrenaline, he dialed Charlotte. This time there was an urgent question that only she could answer. A fact that needed to be checked, so he bypassed the flirting for now.

Drozd led the conversation saying, "Charlotte, I might have something. It may be the direct link to the killer, but I want to make sure to confirm something with you first before I jump to conclusions. Do you remember the school connection you mentioned from your sessions with Shelly?"

She replied, "Yes, of course."

He asked, "When she spoke to you, did she say specifically that he was at the college she attended or do you think it could possibly have been a different school?" The answer to this question could help narrow down the search for the mystery man, the killer.

"There was nothing specific about what school she knew him from in my notes, so yes, that is a possibility. What do you have?"

He was treading on thin ice sharing this much information, but he felt obligated to tell her what he knew, so he did. He started by telling her, "I was in one of the rooms that the murder could have potentially taken place in, searching for clues. There were six rooms in total, I checked. All the rooms were spotless except the next-to-last one. I discovered a small pin or button with an insignia sitting far underneath a nightstand. At the time, I didn't think much about it, but I bagged it anyway. It didn't strike me until just a few minutes ago when I was looking at my board that it might mean something. I have the school connection."

Now things were all falling into place. She made an audible gasp, then said, "Things are definitely getting interesting now."

The breadcrumbs were leading them right to the killer. So many moving pieces on the chess board right now. The lines on the murder board were intersecting. Just a few more moves to checkmate. He could smell the killer, human hunting human, top of the food chain, brain versus brawn. Who was going to claim victory? The scent was strong, and he was moving efficiently, closing in on his prey. This guy was trapped, or so Drozd thought.

They finished their conversation, and Drozd promised that he would keep her updated as the investigation progressed. As he hung up the phone, he was energized because he had never been so sure of his path in life. He was exactly where he wanted to be, doing exactly what he wanted to do, and now he was sure she was exactly who he wanted to get to know because she had a passion for her job just as he did for his. That simple common trait they had attracted him, and it didn't hurt that she looked like Demi Moore, he thought.

182

CHAPTER FIFTY

CHECK

After completing his call with Charlotte Burnett, Detective Drozd immediately dialed Agent Sanford to brief him on the new development and hear about his team's progress.

Sanford answered, "Detective Drozd, how are things progressing in the Mon Valley?"

Drozd replied, "Agent Sanford, a wise man once told me that the small things can sometimes solve a case. I've found something small."

Now Sanford was the one to have his interest piqued as he stood up from his desk, phone cradled to his ear, his other hand on his hip. Sanford said, "What did you find?"

"I was reviewing my whiteboard this morning, looking for that 'small thing' you assigned me to find. I came across a small evidence bag I had completely forgotten about. I found the contents in one of the rooms at the motel where I suspect Shelly was murdered. I wasn't sure if this item was even associated with our crime. It is a little lapel pin with the initials and logo of the California University of Pennsylvania on it, which is located twenty minutes from here."

He had a lot to explain so he continued, "My discovery of this clue preceded the association of Shelly Lynn, her sugar-daddy friend, and school, so I overlooked its significance originally. I only learned of this association of the school after the therapist, Charlotte Burnett, provided information about a session she had with Shelly. She told me Shelly confided to her that the other person in her life had something to do with this school. When Charlotte and I had first spoken about this session, I assumed this association was with someone she went to school with. Therefore, I put my efforts in interviewing teachers, students and even the dean, of the school she attended but made no progress. I concluded it was a dead end after getting no new leads and moved on. I had forgotten about this little pin until this morning I realized I had the tie to the school! It hadn't crossed my mind until I learned the school Shelly spoke to Burnett about might not have been the school she attended. Now it struck me that it wasn't the school she attended but rather the school where the other mystery person either attends or works. I spoke with Burnett just before this call and she confirmed there was no "specific" school mentioned in their session. So now my pin makes sense. The killer dropped it mistakenly at the murder scene and couldn't go back for it when he discovered it was missing or maybe he doesn't know it's missing. I believe our guy works or goes to school there."

Sanford clapped his hands and said, "Well done, my friend. I'm going to keep giving you assignments if you continue to excel at them," he laughed. "We need to work that angle quickly and see who it leads us to. But make no mistake, you should feel good for this victory."

Drozd was proud of his work, but he was also anxious to hear about the progress made by Sanford's team. Drozd then asked "What about your team? Did they make any progress?"

"Well, there is good news and bad news over here. The good news is the Costa Rican authorities woke up today and decided to like us. The bad news is it's going to take twenty-four hours to provide us the list of United States citizens who were in Costa Rica during the time period the murder occurred. Also, they informed us this list was going to be 'mucho large' as they jokingly informed us that period of time was high season for tourists. So, like I said, some good and some bad."

Drozd was a little bit disappointed at this news. He was so close to catching this guy and any slip might cause the game to be lost.

But, he understood that red tape was red tape, and there was nothing they could do except wait anxiously and be prepared to move quickly once they had the information.

Drozd responded, "Our batting average isn't that great today because I was also stonewalled by that website, *LetsDoThis.com*, and their legal counsel. They stated they were 'researching' with their legal team to understand what the website owners' obligations were to their patrons in regards to privacy policies. They closed their response by saying they would try and get back in a 'timely manner.' He continued, "I replied to their email asking, no, almost begging, for a speedy reply. But you know what they say, 'I wouldn't hold my breath on that one.'"

"Well, we are one for three today; that makes our batting average .333. You say that's bad, but in Major League Baseball, it is amazing! Any batter would consider that a career-making year! Let's just agree to look at it that way. And in reality, the fact that we have twenty-four hours before getting that list may be to our advantage. It gives us a chance to get ourselves in place and be ready."

Drozd thought it was amazing that this guy could put such a positive spin on things. Sanford continued, "With that said, let me make a suggestion. I think we need to be working in your location now to make sure we have everything covered and can be ready to move quickly in response to any new developments. My team and I can be on an FBI plane and in Monessen by late afternoon. Would this be acceptable?"

Drozd said excitedly, "The more the merrier. Happy to have the help. This valley could use a more expertly trained team, people with experience handling a situation like this. I would be excited to have you and your team here with me."

Sanford replied, "Good. We will be with you in person later today. Until then can you continue to work that pin and find out what you can about the mystery person at California University of Pennsylvania."

Drozd said, "Got it," and disconnected. He was wired. The last three weeks had resembled the NFL Football Playoffs. The teams involved in the final game; "The Super Bowl," had overcome all obstacles, from opponents to injury, vying to be the last one standing, the ultimate winner. The anticipation of that game would soon be over. Similarly, Drozd had incurred obstacles and hurdles to arrive at this point in his game. It would be over soon the same way, but he had to wait twenty-four hours for this game to begin. Waiting was hard.

He could see the moves to finish the game, it was quite clear. He was confident he was moving to checkmate.

CHAPTER FIFTY-ONE

High Noon

FBI Agent Sanford's team arrived late afternoon as promised. Detective Drozd made space for them in the office. They each set up their work areas with laptops and headsets. Sanford was looking over the murder whiteboard. He thought it was about as complete as he had ever seen. He marveled at Drozd's organizational skills. He liked this guy.

The team went out for dinner. Drozd had taken them to an amazing restaurant called The Back Porch, which was in an old rustic house, situated in a little borough of Charleroi named Speers. It specialized in steaks and other American cuisine, and they had a nice evening getting to know each other better. It helped to pass the time while the team waited for the customs reports from Costa Rica.

At the end of the dinner, Sanford picked up the check saying, "Expense account," as he put down his credit card.

Drozd was still a bit dejected because he didn't make any progress on who the mystery person might be at the California University of Pennsylvania. He didn't have any leads to start with, and because it was a decent-sized campus of about 8,000 students, it was back to the needle-in-the-haystack odds of making progress. The fact that he was not successful wasn't that big of a deal because it was just a matter of time before it would be irrelevant, but Drozd always wanted to excel and succeed.

Tomorrow the team would dig in, when they got the reports from Costa Rica, and quickly research each person individually. Then they would have the name of the killer. On Drozd's murder board, he was still the black silhouette with a question mark under it.

The next morning they assembled at the office. The night before, Sanford had suggested that the team rest up because the next day was going to be a long one. They all were happy for the rest, but Drozd awoke at his normal time and went through his normal morning routine except he added in a five-mile run. After showering, he drove to the office and arrived around nine. Everyone else arrived at around 10:30 and prepared for the day. They were all anxious for the big game to start. They were ready. Now they just looked up at the clock on the wall.

At 11:52, Sanford's computer made an audible "ding," signaling an email had arrived. Drozd and Sanford both looked up and quickly moved to his laptop. They clicked on the email icon and began scanning it.

Here we go, thought Drozd!

Subject line: Male U.S. Citizens in San Jose, Costa Rica. May 15, 2008.

It was a very long list, just as the customs officials had inferred. It had over 1,250 names on it. Once he was ready, Sanford called out instructions to his team. He quickly assigned them portions of the list. He was giving them ten names at a time to check the passport addresses and then cross reference where they said they would be staying while in Costa Rica. This was going to be a daunting task, but the team could handle it. Sanford was managing them and Drozd was pacing nervously. It took about two hours before there was something that fit. A name that had a listed address as Monogahela, Pennsylvania, and the place of stay while in Costa Rica was none other than The Del Ray Hotel: Robert Reynolds! There was the mystery man, their ghost. He had made a mistake!

The team was very excited but Sanford kept them in check, saying, "I need everything listed by Costa Rica customs on this person of interest, please," assigning it to one of his team, David Swaze. He went right to work, typing feverishly with query for advanced searches on this individual.

Analyst David Swaze called to his boss about 15 minutes later. "I have everything on this guy, sir," he said, glancing up from his computer screen. He provided him with the background on Robert Reynolds quickly and efficiently.

Robert Reynolds aka Bobby Reynolds - Place of stay: Hotel Del Ray, San Jose, Costa Rica. Arrival: May 13, 2008. Departure: May 16, 2008. The timeline was perfect, but Sanford still wasn't completely satisfied. While the team member was gathering the information on Reynolds he had the rest of the team checking all other names on that list to make sure there weren't any other potential matches. Sanford wanted to be thorough.

Sanford was typing on his laptop, feverishly trying to find a present address from the Department of Motor Vehicles for Robert Reynolds. At the same time, Drozd was searching "Robert Reynolds" on Google. He found some helpful information: born Monogahela, Pennsylvania, 1965, Charleroi Hospital. Attended college at IUP, the abbreviation for Indiana University of Pennsylvania, where he lettered in football for the IUP Hawks. It had a list of the places he taught in his career. Saint Vincent University, Latrobe Pennsylvania, 1988-1993; University of South

Carolina, Columbia, South Carolina, 1994-1998; University of Texas at Austin, Austin, Texas, 1999-2003; And lastly, California University of Pennsylvania, 2004 to the present. There were also some articles about his proficiency for competitive urban assault pistol competitions.

Drozd said, "Look at this!" as he showed the articles to Sanford. Now Drozd understood why the murders were all over the country. Reynolds was a professor and had worked at several universities.

"Gotcha!" exclaimed Sanford, for two reasons. One, they had the *means* and *opportunity* proof needed to build a strong case. Reynolds was documented to be in the area at the times of all of the murders. Two, they were pretty sure of the *motive*, a scorned boyfriend kills his ex-girlfriend's daughter in revenge of something that happened long ago, an *indiscretion*. They could piece this together based on the information Ms. Johnson provided about her son Danny's affair with Shelly's mother, Terri. All the other crimes would have to match this profile, but it would take some time to completely prove that out.

Sanford was multitasking as he listened to Drozd, finding the address for Reynolds through the Department of Motor Vehicles. He was still giving commands to his team, stating, "I need to know everything about this guy. I want to know him better than his own mother!"

Now they needed to start making the plan to apprehend him.

Drozd could see his opponent's king exposed in the chess game. It was time to finish it.

CHAPTER FIFTY-TWO

RELIEF EFFORTS

Dan Holiday wrote:

Hello Dr. Burnett. I hope the day finds you well. I feel my therapy is coming to an end and I am healed! You are amazing! Things have been progressing along well and my work will soon be done. Then I can find my peace. You have been a part of my plan since I found out that you were treating Shelly. She confided to me about your wonderful sessions, so I decided to see how I could benefit from treatment too.

Doc, I've been honest with you every single time we exchange information. But after analysis, what I received was four months of this gibberish being spit back at me. You're capable of much better work, in my opinion. What you gave me were canned responses designed to keep me paying my monthly fee. But I did listen to your responses and tried my best to squeeze anything out of them in regards to understanding why I am the way I am. Instead of your treatment making me want to change, I've just become more accepting of who I am. The world on the other hand might not look so kindly upon me for being that person. You see Dr. Burnett, I kill.

I kill people. I don't carry any ill will towards the people I kill, but at some point, they all broke that moral code you spoke of in our session. Okay, maybe I lied in that statement a bit. To be accurate, I did have ill will towards some of these people. That's better, a clarified more accurate statement because I already told you that I don't lie to you. But that's not here nor there, right? I try and give the people I kill respect after they die. I make sure they are clean and tidy. I place them in spots where they can look gently into eternity. Poetic isn't it, Doctor?

I was so happy that you could help Shelly. She was a wonderful person, but maybe just a bit too consumed with what she had in this life. She was my ultimate cherry on top of the sundae. She represented the last piece of a big plan. The pain I have will be gone soon. I'm sure Shelly's mother, Terri, is now feeling the pain of her loss. The loss of innocence is the true loss in our world. She lost what was most important to her in this world. I lost the essence of myself because of her actions. It's a fair trade, I think. That's when I created my moral code of what I deem acceptable.

Not to put salt in the wound Doc, but if you had examined our sessions a little bit closer, you would have realized that everything was right there for you to know what I am. I was right in front of you in plain sight, but alas, you could not see me.

Rule number one: Always do the job right the first time. Perfection is attainable, and I did this in my work.

Rule number two: Get up early and work until the job is done. The job may take up to five years to do correctly and I am a man who stays on schedule. I always refer back to rule number one.

Rule number three: Degradation is a strong motivator. Use that to adhere to rules one and two as motivation to plan the job well and get it done right the first time.

Rule number four: Put up your barrier to protect yourself. By whatever means necessary keep your feelings numb. Well, to be honest, rule number three takes care of this.

Rule number five: Realize that you are nothing. You are small in the eyes of all who are watching. Being close to nothing makes you easy to overlook and easy to hide in plain sight.

These were our lessons, Dr. Burnett. This will probably make you rethink being involved with this online therapy platform since I know you are an intelligent person. But I am the wake-up call for what can go wrong with a system driven by money and profits. I'm sure being part of that system and me exposing your lackadaisical work makes your blood boil a bit. It actually makes me laugh.

I am fine knowing that everyone got what they deserved as I leave. I won't be back. I am standing here in the same place as Rocky Balboa stood after conquering the stairs, metaphorically of course. Now you can picture me being on top of those stairs in Philadelphia, overlooking the city, and claiming victory over all of my demons. I have conquered the stairs, overcame all adversity, and my arms are stretched above over my head. I know that I have succeeded. Just like Rocky. You should picture me with my arms up Doc. Oops, you have never seen me, my bad.

Take care of yourself. I know if you could have seen my eyes you would have known who I am, but that is why this arrangement worked out so well.
Yours truly, Dan Holiday

P.S. Okay maybe a little white lie on my name. You get it, from the movie, Tombstone. Doc Holiday. His quotes in the movie are just classic. "Play for blood that's just my game!" The other one I love is, "My hypocrisy goes only so far!" These are my words to live by Doc!

Holiday thought for a moment and then said to himself, *You'll know my name soon, Dr. Burnett. But I don't want to give it away too early and deny you the lesson of delayed gratification. Patience.*

CHAPTER FIFTY-THREE

Doc Shock

Therapist Charlotte Burnett opened the email from her patient Dan Holiday. It had been delivered late last evening, but she didn't check her inbox until later in the afternoon. She was not quick enough. She saw who it was from and casually clicked on the icon to open the email. Her mouth dropped, and she gasped, "Oh, fuck, what have I done?" As she was reading it, she turned pale white, her fists clinched, and a splitting headache started as her heart rate spiked. She desperately reached for her phone to call Detective Drozd. She dialed his number as fast as her fingers could move, misdialing on her first try. She was shaking, her mind racing from thought to thought. She was asking herself if she had seen and read it when it was delivered if it could have made a difference. Was this guy going to kill again and wanted to be caught? Could she stop it? The sickening feeling of helplessness was in her chest as she succumbed to the weight of the words in the email.

She was shaking but managed to dial Drozd. "Fuck," she shouted after it rang five times and went to voicemail. She tried again and again but to no avail, eventually realizing the attempts were futile. She sat down in the chair and started to cry. *How did this happen?* Quickly she reviewed the path of the treatment. She had been working with this client for four months. She thought they were making progress. He had just seemed like a normal, emotional guy. She could see now he was exactly the opposite. He was, just like he said, hiding in plain sight.

This was exactly why not seeing a patient's face and their reactions during sessions would never work. The protocols screamed failure, actually bordering on malpractice. This text-and-response methodology of treatment was simply about the money. She vowed that this was the last job that tied her hands behind her back like this. Sure, the owners of this online therapy platform could charge less because a read and response analysis could be accomplished in five minutes instead of a fifty-minute live session. Additionally, they had no lease cost for office space. But at what consequence to the patients? Now she knew exactly—people's lives were ended and the impact would reverberate through all those that cared for the victims forever. All of it could have been prevented.

She put her fingers on her temples and began to rub them to try and relieve some of the pressure. She knew that really wasn't going to help but it was a reaction to the stress and pain she was feeling.

CHAPTER FIFTY-FOUR

HERE WE GO!

It was a school day so they needed to get eyes on him and take him where he would be around the least amount of civilians. They definitely did not want to apprehend him at the school with a full campus of potential casualties. There were already so many school shootings in the news that people were at their wits end with paranoia about it. They decided on the best course of action for the take down: his house was the best location to try to apprehend him. Agent Sanford's team had quickly researched the area and found that it was far away from the congested areas of Monongahela. Bobby Reynolds lived in the house he had grown up in. He inherited it when his parents passed away. It sat on an acre and his closest neighbor was on the other side of the acre. There was no information indicating anyone else resided with him.

The first thing they did was insert a female undercover officer at California University after getting permission from the Dean and coordinating with the school's security department.

The undercover officer alerted the team when Reynolds was leaving for the day. He made his way to his Toyota Tacoma which was parked in the professors' lot, in his spot, marked with his name. This perk made him feel like he was someone special. He threw his briefcase on the passenger seat and started the ignition. He pulled out and proceeded onto the road for the seventeen-minute trip home. He did not notice the unmarked cars rotating tailing him all the way home. First one would follow, then break off, while another took its place so as not to raise Reynolds' suspicion.

During the drive home Reynolds' brain drifted to thoughts of Shelly and their last encounter. She had been the perfect "sugar baby." He could afford her monthly stipend. The weekly meetings were the highlight of his lonely days, making him feel alive again. He was so thankful no one had ever learned about their arrangement. He did start to have feelings for her as they spent more time together. In the days after the murder he felt very lucky that no one had come to speak with him about it and their relationship. If it had come out he was having this type of relationship he might have lost his position at the college, and he was coming up for tenure next year. He was thankful that he had given Shelly the money in cash to pay for the room that night. No one had ever actually seen him enter or leave the motel. He wondered what would have happened if he hadn't left suddenly because a neighbor phoned informing him there was a suspicious car parked outside his house and that he should check on it. Shelly might still have been alive. This made him sad. But maybe he could try again with a different girl.

He used his garage door opener and pulled in. He clicked the opener again to close the garage door. He walked into his house, moving into his kitchen to put his briefcase on the table. He was going to prepare a simple meal of chicken, rice, and vegetables before preparing his lectures for the next day.

When the garage door closed, the cars transporting all the agents pulled slowly up to the curb. Detective Drozd was in an SUV with Agent Sanford. They were sure that Reynolds had not seen them during the drive to his house. Now they had him trapped inside. They opened the door and exited the vehicle. The other agents from Sanford's team also exited their cars. The Southwestern Pennsylvania State Police Department SWAT team parked a short distance away and got out and into position. They were ready to apprehend Reynolds. Agent Sanford was running point on this operation, and he made sure everyone knew the rules of engagement.

Sanford checked that everyone understood their assignments before they started to move to get into position. He tested radio communications and made sure everyone had their body armor on. All weapons were checked and double-checked. They moved two snipers into strategic locations covering both the front and back entrances. Other officers and agents were situated throughout the property. Drozd and Sanford used the SUV for cover and also concealment. They were all in place.

It had taken them about ten minutes to get everyone into position as the teams had to move slowly to avoid drawing attention or detection. Sanford asked his snipers if they had a situation report. They both communicated there was no movement at either door. They also said there was no movement from neighbors or car traffic. This was about as good as it was going to get. It was time to make their move.

Sanford asked Drozd if there was anything else he wanted done before they moved in.

Drozd said, "No, sir."

Sanford reached into the SUV and grabbed ahold of the handset of the loudspeaker system built into the vehicle. He spoke into the microphone.

The chess match was almost over. Drozd didn't think the killer had anymore moves left.

CHAPTER FIFTY-FIVE

GOODBYE MY FRIENDS IT'S HARD TO DIE

Reynolds heard his phone ring. He didn't recognize the number. He was relaxed and decided to answer, his mind drifting about what would be on TV tonight.

A voice asked, "Hello, Bobby. How are you on this fine day?"

Reynolds asked, "Who is this?"

"Well Bobby, I'm from your distant past. I am calling today to give you something that is long overdue."

Reynolds said agitatedly, "I don't have time for this shit today, man!"

"Bobby, you don't have any choice in this matter!"

Reynolds was truly perplexed. Was this a joke or prank? No matter what, he was getting pissed and started to speak again but was abruptly cut off.

The person interjected with a startling authority. "No joke! No prank! Just shut the fuck up and listen until I'm finished speaking," he said flatly, "or I'll end you now! You see, Bobby, the reason I'm calling is because today is a day of reckoning! I'm not even sure if you are aware what that is, but in easy-to-understand terms, it's time to atone for your sins!"

Reynolds interjected, "What fucking sins, man?"

The caller shot back, "I said shut the fuck up! And don't even think about hanging up because for you the consequences are much worse than listening to me!" He continued, "Now back to our story, we don't have much time. A long time ago you took something from me. I don't think you even knew you did it. Maybe you did know and maybe it gave you a chuckle. But I have paid for it every day since. So now I am here to collect the debt you owe me." The person paused.

Reynolds started to speak, then held his tongue, trying to think what he had done and how to get himself out of this.

The person started speaking again. "Bobby, there are FBI agents and SWAT officers surrounding your house. Please feel free to look, but if I were you, I wouldn't put your head too close to any windows for any extended period of time because one of those snipers or agents may punch your ticket with a quick trigger finger. Understand, I have spent years leading them to you, directly to you." His voice was calm and calculated with no inflection. "You can be one hundred percent sure that they are coming for you for six murders and more."

"Murders? What fucking murders?"

"Shut the fuck up!" the man fired back. "I have made sure you won't want to go with them because of the consequences that are waiting for you. You see, I was the one who placed those pop-ups on your computer. You know the ones from LetsDoThis.com, Hotel Del Ray, and HelpYouNow.com, which I hid from you but now have made viewable for the authorities to find. You were so easy to manipulate. I especially liked sharing Shelly's link from LetsDoThis.com with you so you would have the perfect opportunity to start an affair, which of course you did. You didn't even remember her mom, Terri. Do you realize that you made love to both a mother and her daughter? Talk about keeping it in the family—and quite a feat by most men's standards. It was very easy to gain access to your computer to help you, guide you, and tempt you. That was the beginning of the plan, but I took it a little further to ensure the results I wanted. Sadly, I admit I have behaved badly. I placed some really nasty pictures and videos of child pornography on the hard drive of your computer for those nice agents to find. Believe me they will find it, because I didn't work very hard to hide it."

Reynolds wanted to speak but the voice kept cutting him off, making him feel small and weak.

The killer's voice finally showed enthusiasm. "You've been perfectly set up to be the fall guy for killing six people! I took painstaking steps to provide the authorities all the evidence they need to convict you. They have it all: means, motive, and opportunity for every murder. You are fucked, and you will be convicted. The proof is absolute, so you will either go to jail or face the death penalty! I expect they will seek the death penalty because all of the murders were premeditated. I know because I planned them well in advance and carried them out personally. You know what they say, if you want something done right, do it yourself," he finished, laughing.

Reynolds began to sweat and started to feel sick to his stomach. This guy was fucking crazy but it sounded like everything he was saying was legitimate. Was it possible? He didn't know of any murders he spoke about except for Shelly.

The killer continued, "Now let's examine your options. It's simple. Go to jail and be killed by other inmates for the child pornography because they don't tolerate that type of indiscretion. They will undoubtedly rape you and make you do unfathomable things before you are shanked in the shower. You could also die by lethal injection after being convicted for six murders in the first degree. That's a pleasant ending. Or behind door number three, you have the option to just kill yourself right now which will save you a lot of pain! These aren't the best of options but they are the only ones available. I know you have guns in the house and are quite good with them. The authorities know that also so they won't hesitate to put you down. It's not a stretch of the imagination to think that you are capable of shooting yourself in the head. Let me guess, you're trying to figure out how to get out of this right now. Maybe you'll just tell the authorities about this conversation. It's not going to work because this is a burner phone so nobody will ever know about this conversation nor believe your story."

Reynolds said, "You're fucking crazy, there's no one out there," peeking out through the window. But to his chagrin, there were some strange vehicles lined up along the road. They looked vaguely familiar, especially the large black SUV. *What the fuck?* How had his life come to this? How could he get out of this? His mind was racing, and he was feeling sick. He was thinking about what he should do. *Was this guy telling the truth about all the evidence? Why me?* He wasn't rich, so it couldn't be money. He knew this Shelly arrangement was immoral but not illegal. Had he fucked with the wrong person? He was trying to figure the way out of this, but he knew he was trapped with no best case scenario, just bad outcomes.

The killer said, "Hey, Bobby, snap out of it, you don't have much time! They are coming for you now. It's time to act or face the consequences. We all have to go sometime. You are just going to get to the finish line earlier than you expected. Well, I've got to go—it's been so nice playing this game with you. Bye-bye."

The connection went dead.

Reynolds thought quickly. He didn't want to go to jail only to be killed, raped, or suffer other brutalities. In shock, he slowly made his way into his bedroom. His hands were trembling but he managed to punch the code into his gun safe and took out his gun. He made sure a round was chambered and he knew the magazine was full. He put it under his chin, shaking uncontrollably. But he just couldn't do it. He couldn't pull the trigger even though he knew his life was over. He didn't want to die, but he also couldn't see a way out.

Over a loudspeaker a voice spoke, "Robert Reynolds we have a warrant for your arrest. Please exit the house with your hands up." He knew what had to be done. He stood up, put the gun in his hand, flipped the safety off, and charged the pistol.

He opened the door and ran out firing at the sky. All the SWAT and FBI agents opened fire at the threat of the gunfire.

Once the firing stopped, Drozd ran to Reynolds. Upon arrival he carefully kicked the gun far away from his reach to eliminate any potential danger. He could see Reynold's eyes were still open as he gasped for air. There was a trickle of blood coming out of his mouth. Drozd could see he was trying to verbalize something, so he knelt next to him and put his ear close to Reynold's mouth, straining to hear his words. They were too soft to understand, and it was too late because this was his last breath. Drozd could make out the first of two words started with an *N* but the rest was inaudible. He watched as the eyes of the killer turned from alive to the mucky color of death. What had he said? Drozd would never know, but it would haunt him for a long time.

Reynolds died by the law enforcement firing squad. He was shot over twenty times and was later pronounced dead at the scene by the paramedics who arrived minutes later. No one would ever know about the conversation that occurred just one hundred and twenty seconds before the end of his life. The reckoning was complete.

CHAPTER FIFTY-SIX

Clean Up

There was a lot to do at the scene. Everyone from both teams pitched in—some helping to cordon the area off and mark it as a crime scene, and others on evidence collection. There would be a lot of work to do to search this property thoroughly. Inside the house Agent Sanford had organized the team, and they started sweeping from room to room looking for anything that might be evidence in the murder investigations. A forensics team would come shortly, but this initial search was important. A little over an hour into the search, one team member found something in a ventilation duct in a spare bedroom. It was a gun in a small gun case—a .22 magnum pistol with an unattached silencer. Hopefully it was to the weapon used for all the murders. Other items were discovered that were likely used in the murders such as plastic rip-ties, elastic bands, and rubber gloves.

Checkmate. The king was knocked over.

The media started to arrive not long after the call for the ambulance. The members of the SWAT team had originally been in charge of the exterior of the crime scene until local law enforcement arrived and took over. The news station had sent one person but upon arrival they saw the extent of the law enforcement presence and called for reinforcements. Within an hour there were reporters and TV cameras vying for the best vantage point to get footage and information. Law enforcement officers kept them at arm's length and the scene under control.

As Detective Drozd and Agent Sanford exited the house, they carried the evidence bags containing the gun and what law enforcement referred to as a "kill bag." The bag's contents consisted of rip-ties, plastic gloves, and elastic bands. They also gathered up Bobby Reynolds' phone and laptop for analysis. Sanford's team could find anything there was to find on digital storage devices like these. They hoped they might find the motive, means, and opportunity for all the other murder cases. There was still work to be done to fully understand it all, but with the murder weapon in hand, they were positive they had their man.

The reporters, lined up outside the cordoned area, tried to get their attention, but Drozd and Sanford waved them off. There would be a time to let the public know, but not now. The reporters were not amused to be shunned, but the local police did their job and kept everything orderly.

Forensics units took over after Drozd, Sanford, and the team felt they had found as much as they were capable. They had successfully closed the case by stopping the killer and finding damning evidence. As they walked out the door, they saw the EMTs loading the body bag containing Bobby Reynolds into the ambulance. They pulled out unceremoniously and drove away. There was no need for the siren because he was declared deceased two hours ago.

Sanford sent his team back to the hotel. He rode with Drozd. They stopped at his office first to put the evidence into the locker for safekeeping. Then they went to a local pub and shared a pitcher of beer. They deserved it. They needed to take the edge off. Their adrenaline levels would probably crash soon, leavingech of them with a giant headache, so they figured they might as well add to it with a few beers. They talked about everything and nothing. Sometimes they spoke about the case and other times about their personal lives.

After a few beers, Drozd confided that he was curious about the therapist, Charlotte Burnett on a personal level, and he mentioned she told him that she looked like Demi Moore.

Sanford raised an eyebrow and said "Man, I think you are going to have to research that and confirm it with cold hard facts. I want to know the results." They both laughed heartily.

Drozd pulled out his phone and turned it back on. It had been off since the operation started in the afternoon because he wanted to be focused. When his phone started, he saw he had numerous missed calls from Charlotte. He dialed quickly, and she picked up on the very first ring.

Drozd said, "Charlotte, are you okay?"

She quickly blurted out, "Far from it!"

She said, "I blew it Bill."

"Blew what?" he asked. She continued, "I couldn't save them."

Drozd tried to calm her, saying, "Charlotte, start from the beginning."

She told him about the email from Dan Holiday, and not opening it until later in the afternoon. She sounded numb as she started to read the email word for word.

When she finished Drozd broke in saying, "Charlotte we got him!" He shared that the case broke open based on the international information. He told her how invaluable her help with Shelly's sessions had been.

When she heard these praises she seemed to ease up and relax. They mutually agreed that in a couple weeks he would take a trip to Silver Springs for a nice evening of food and conversation. He said they had to because he had a research project given to him that only she could help with. They disconnected but both were excited about their upcoming rendezvous. Wow, he had a date! Sanford had assigned him the job to research whether she indeed looked like Demi Moore. It would be well worth the four-and-a-half hour drive.

For the first time in his life he knew he was on the right path. He thrived on his work being challenging and rewarding. He had met someone that made him re-evaluate the importance of aspects of his life. But he also knew he would not be able to stay in Monessen much longer.

Drozd and Sanford went back to Drozd's office after the pub. Drozd noticed he had a new email. They wondered what could be coming in so late in the evening but then realized in Europe where LetsDoThis.com was headquartered, it was already the next morning.

Drozd started to read it to Sanford:

> From: info@LetsDoThis.com
>
> Subject Line: Name
>
> Detective Drozd, after all legal and moral aspects were examined, our company has decided to give you the name of the individual that contacted Shelly Lynn based on the mitigating circumstance of her death. It was Robert Reynolds. We hope this helps your investigation. Should

you need more assistance with his billing address or access to the data exchanges that occurred between them while on our site, please contact me personally.

Drozd looked up at Sanford and stated, "Better late than never!" They knew the evidence against Reynolds was overwhelming, and they were glad to get him off the streets.

There was a ton of paperwork to be done but they sat and tried to figure out how this whole thing had stayed quiet for so long. All those cases had common threads that no one linked together. Each murder was perfectly spaced. And in the email to therapist Burnett, Reynolds basically confessed everything. That email would help them tie everything up neatly in the days to come. They were exhausted and a little inebriated. But all and all they were feeling pretty good.

CHAPTER FIFTY-SEVEN

WAVE TO SAND

Detective Drozd needed a good night's sleep. He hadn't slept soundly in two weeks. Once the adrenaline was gone, he crashed with a terrible headache. The pitcher of beer with Agent Sanford might have contributed to this headache. It was no wonder he fell into a deep sleep and that sleep took the pain away by the next morning. Thankfully, last night he had no dreams of being chased or chasing, which was a blessing.

He had been on the hunt. It took everything he had to find this predator. The predator had turned out to be hiding within the flock. This allowed him to stay invisible for a long time. That is exactly what it said in the letter from Dan Holiday, alias Bobby Reynolds. He admitted it all. It was as if he wanted them to know that he was smarter than they were.

Drozd got up and made coffee, then went for a run. Later he showered and got dressed knowing that he was in for a tough, emotional visit to the actual target, although not physical target of the killings, Terri Lynn. He hoped that she would never know to what extent she was responsible for the death of her only child. Now he thought about how to speak about their findings without revealing the true motive for Shelly's death.

He called Terri Lynn asking if it was okay to stop by this morning, and if it was, what time would be convenient. Terri said she was not going out in a monotone, matter-of-fact voice. With the events that had transpired, she would not face the world today or any day soon.

The television news crews and reporters from various papers had been relentless overnight as they stationed themselves outside her house. The media somehow got information about the events that occurred at Reynolds' house. He had been identified as the killer of Shelly and other victims. They were poised to capture any sighting of Terri. They wanted her story badly. She wasn't cooperating, not speaking or showing herself. They stayed overnight and waited patiently. They were all there for one reason: to get the exclusive interview with the victim's mother.

Drozd drove to Bentleyville. He was mentally running through what he planned to tell Terri. So far, he hadn't come up with any good way to provide her the facts. She needed to hear the truth about what had transpired and some bits of information that led up to the ending that occurred.

Today was the first day the sun disappeared. November weather was unpredictable both in temperature and amount of sunlight in Mon Valley. This was the first overcast day with a slight chill in the air. It wasn't cold, nor warm, but somewhere in the middle. The overcast condition matched the gloomy feeling that events of the previous day had left on the valley. Drozd didn't even pay attention to the weather conditions. His mind was elsewhere during the twenty-two-minute drive in absolute quiet. He did not even turn on the radio for distraction, instead savored the solitude. This calm was something that Drozd was desperately in need of before meeting with Terri.

As he got close to her home, reporters and cameramen, journalists, and onlookers made a beeline toward his vehicle. He took a straight line right toward the house and waved off their requests. First, he thought, *vultures*, as they circled and waited. Then he thought, *they are just doing their jobs*.

He exited his car and walked up the stairs as Terri opened the door. As he entered, she gestured toward the living room, and he walked in and sat down on a chair. She sat across from him on the couch.

He said, "Let me start again by telling you how sorry I am for everything that has happened to you."

She thanked him but seemed a million miles away.

He started to explain how they had found Bobby Reynolds. Terri's eyes darted up at the mention of that name. Drozd didn't mention that Bobby was the source of Shelly's new income, but he was sure it would come out soon. He also explained how they ruled out Gavin Dean, and shared the timeline and how the trail had led them from Danny Johnson to her daughter's horrible murder.

He immediately sensed her unease as she stood up abruptly and started to pace and sway as if actually hearing some melody. Her arms were crossed and she stared at him blankly, looking straight through him.

Drozd told her about the five other cases pending, one of them was the murder of Danny Johnson. He said that the authorities had always thought Danny was the victim of a drug deal gone awry. But now they knew better.

Terri was mortified by the two familiar names Drozd had mentioned: Bobby Reynolds and Danny Johnson. Immediately, he could see her lose all the color from her face. She never thought that period of her life would come to light. Drozd asked if there was someone he could call to support her. She shook it off and remained standing, swaying back and forth as if recalling something.

Drozd said, "We know for a fact that Bobby Reynolds was a sociopath, killing people undetected for the last twenty-five years. We don't know why he targeted your daughter exactly." He was lying. He knew what the truth was, in fact it was designed to hurt Terri forever. Drozd thought there was no need to pile guilt of her daughter's death directly on her shoulders. The email to therapist Burnett had outlined Reynolds' motive and how he had hidden right in front of everyone.

Terri blurted out, "I dated Bobby when I was young!" Tears were now streaming down her face. "He was a football player, and I had a relationship with him. I also dated Danny. He was just a boy I knew from town, but I spent time with him also. But why did he kill Terri?" she asked in a pleading voice. "Did Bobby kill Danny?" she asked.

"Terri, did your relationship with Bobby end badly?"

She replied "Do any relationships ever really end well? It lasted about six months and the situation just wasn't working for me. I was actually dating someone else at the time. He was the one who was really upset when he found out. But Bobby never spoke to me again. Why would he do this to Shelly?"

That made sense. It sounded like Danny was upset because Terri was dating Bobby. He didn't want to dig deeper into this memory because of her fragile state of mind, so he let it go.

Drozd replied, "We haven't sorted it all out yet, but there has been a number of victims since. They date back to the 1980s, including Danny."

He didn't mention the names of the other victims but gave her as much information as he could about everything else. He stayed until she became less emotional. They talked for another twenty minutes about the actual attempt to arrest Bobby. He informed her that the incident went sideways when Bobby came out brandishing a gun. The officers were attempting to bring him into custody and had to defend themselves when he started shooting.

Before leaving, he hugged her lightly but he didn't think she felt it. They separated, shook hands, and said goodbye. As he left, he looked back and saw her crying with her head on the kitchen table. Her life was forever changed.

It was challenging dodging all of the reporters to get back to his car. He kept his head down, climbed into his car and backed down the driveway. He turned onto the road that lead back to Monessen. The reporters would get their chance to ask questions about the investigation at the 2:00 press conference at police headquarters.

CHAPTER FIFTY-EIGHT

CHECKMATE

The mayor was the center of attention. News crews from all Pittsburgh area television stations were represented, in addition to area print media outlets. Catching such a prolific killer was big news not only locally but also nationally. The mayor offered his gratitude to Detective Drozd, FBI Agent Sanford and team, and everyone else who assisted with the investigation.

"I give southwestern Pennsylvania's deepest gratitude to these two amazing men: Detective Bill Drozd from the Monessen Police Department, and Special Agent Carlos Sanford from the Federal Bureau of Investigation," said the mayor. There was some applause and then he gestured for quiet. He continued, "These two men were able to do what they did only through deep dedication and skillful execution. Now we as a community are safer! Agent Sanford, will you answer a few questions?" the mayor asked.

Agent Sanford came to the podium, cleared his throat slightly, and replied, "Detective Drozd brought it to the FBI's attention that there might be an individualwho had been taking the lives of innocent people for many years. He needed help more on a national and international level to confirm his theory." My team just followed up the leads, and through hard work and dedication, not to mention the great investigative work of Detective Drozd, we were lucky to succeed in stopping this individual from ever hurting another person."

When asked about the attempted apprehension of Robert Reynolds, Agent Sanford stated, "We tried our best to take Mr. Reynolds into custody with no bloodshed. He was given a chance to cooperate. He decided not to follow our instructions, and with his actions, he endangered the lives of the good law enforcement officers who were tasked with the job of taking him into custody. With that said, the officers took action, and unfortunately Mr. Reynolds was killed after brandishing and firing a weapon. Fortunately, none of our team nor any civilians were injured."

With that the Mayor stepped in and shook Agent Sanford's hand, thanking him once again. The mayor then introduced Detective Bill Drozd who moved up to the podium. "Folks this is southwestern Pennsylvania Detective Bill Drozd who led this investigation from start to finish," exclaimed the Mayor.

Before the mediator assigned someone to ask a question, Detective Drozd put up his finger and spoke first.

"Before your questions I wanted to thank Agent Sanford and his team. But I also want to add a thanks to Therapist Charlotte Burnett who provided invaluable insight and information to the investigation helping us tremendously. I consider us a team now and together we got lucky and had a positive outcome to this tragedy." Now he nodded to the mediator.

A journalist from a prominent newspaper asked Drozd, "What was the turning point in the case?"

Detective Drozd, replied "We connected this individual to all the locations where the murders had been committed.

We had evidence to support motive, intent, and means, which made us one hundred percent confident that we have the right person.

The interview went on for another fifteen minutes with Drozd and Sanford fielding questions to which their answers were concise and calculated.

When it concluded, exchanges of handshakes were flowing, and the mood was elevated.

Far away the killer watched the press conference on his television. When he heard Drozd say he was 100% confident they had the right person, he laughed and almost fell over in delight. He said to himself, "Checkmate Detective Drozd."

How beautiful this whole adventure had turned out. Everyone who deserved to die was dead. The blame for all these deaths lay directly on Robert Reynolds, who also was now dead. Lastly, and most important, he was free and clear to start his life again.

"What a good job I did!" he said to himself aloud. He was proud of himself.

He didn't hear another word, he tuned it all out. He was thinking back to his moment on the stairs in Philadelphia and pictured himself with raised hands above his head in triumph, the celebratory pose of Rocky Balboa.

The killer had everything he needed and got in the car and left. He didn't plan on returning anytime soon. He was done. It was time to relax. Maybe he would find "the one," but he wasn't counting on it.

CHAPTER FIFTY-NINE

JUST BUSINESS

He was a street kid, a product of his experiences. African American, tall and lean, he very rarely smiled but had an intensity visible in his eyes and his gestures that left a lasting impression. He never really had much of a chance in life, growing up in the projects of Donora. He didn't have many advantages and did what he had to do to survive. Once he had a small amount of hope when he was playing high school football but that was taken away when he failed to keep his grades at an acceptable level. It resulted in his suspension from the team until he could comply with the school guidelines. There was no chance that would ever happen.

He met her when she accompanied her friend to meet him and "get some supplies"—a nicer way of saying acquiring drugs. The women met him in the park and he was immediately attracted to the smaller woman. She flirted and acted tough, which he found exciting. He boasted about his "lucrative" business and what it afforded him, including advantages he could provide if she wanted to spend time with him. Without saying it directly, he wanted to have sex with her in exchange for drugs, money, or anything else she deemed a fair trade. He was determined to succeed and get what he wanted.

She resisted in the beginning, claiming she had a boyfriend. He jabbed back, boasting about the size of his manhood, and the benefits he could provide were large also. He was six years older than she and that excited her. He wore her down, and when they finished their conversation, it was determined that the next weekend was when their rendezvous would take place. They met on a Thursday and did not reappear until Sunday, each getting what they needed from the experience.

His name was Danny Johnson.

CHAPTER SIXTY

THE BALL IS IN YOUR COURT

Julie was a 33-year-old brown-haired, green-eyed beauty. She was 5'7" and had a perfect smile. She was very pretty in the eyes of everyone around her, and the majority of men would have given a limb to have just one night with her. She lived in Greensburg, Pennsylvania, 30 miles southeast of Pittsburgh. Greensburg is within the Laurel Highlands area, and there are many things to do there due to the economically affluent population.

Julie worked at the Greensburg Racquet Club. It was a nice facility with an exclusive clientele from the Greensburg and Ligonier areas which were very affluent. She coordinated schedules, answered phones, and worked in the small pro shop that sold clothing and supplies.

She never had a bad word for anyone—always a kind word or friendly smile. She had become despondent and had confided to friends that her boyfriend was being less than attentive. She had met him years ago at the racquet club. He played often and eventually flirted with her enough to get her phone number. It didn't take long before they were dating and getting closer. She had fallen in love with him and hoped that he would ask her to marry him, but he had not even hinted at that. She thought the world of him. Now he seemed distant, coming to the club less and less. He seem to focus more on work and running off to the ski resort for his so-called "escape trips" without her. She viewed this as him trying to create distance between them.

Every time she asked him about it he would say, "I get stressed at work and I need to release it." She thought there was much more to it than that.

She was worried that morning because he would always check in with a quick call. But morning and afternoon went by, and when he didn't call the entire night, she called the Seven Springs Ski Resort Lodge where he was staying.

His name was Elliot Kidd.

CHAPTER SIXTY-ONE

So Many Men So Little Time

She had met him in town and treated him like her uncle. But it crossed the line into a forbidden affair after a night of alcohol. The relationship had started as a mentorship but became more. She didn't look at it that way, but he did. He knew of her reputation but thought by showing her how good it could be she would choose him.

She looked at it differently and told him, "Sex is just sex. It feels good. Just enjoy me," she implored him. "Enjoy my body. Life is short." This worked for him because in the past he never got emotionally involved with people. This trait simplified his life because he liked to remain invisible. He had done a good job to keep all of those emotions in order allowing him to stay on track and achieving his ultimate desired outcome. That was until she started flaunting her lack of moral right and wrong right in his face.

Once she flirted with another guy in a bar while they were having a drink. She gave the guy her phone number right in front of him. She danced with the other suitor and then came back to sit down with him. He had simply gotten up and walked out, never seeing her again. That had been two years before her demise. It was just long enough to make sure there was no trace of them ever being together.

After the killer ended her life, he simply faded way, again.

Her name was Stacy Collins.

CHAPTER SIXTY-TWO

BRAGGERS BALL

He was having drinks with friends and became totally inebriated, to understate it. It was in a dive bar where the beer was cold and the music was from his era, so it made for a fun atmosphere. He had a high-pressure job, and once in a while he had to let loose. Too many failures at work, no matter what the excuse, would inevitably lead to being fired. At his job, your stock only went up when you succeeded. Winners got the advantages and got paid more. But this night he needed to just be one of the boys.

Boy's locker room talk always revolved around two things: cars and women. Okay, mostly women. Who had you slept with? Whether the woman was young, old, attractive, not attractive, it just didn't matter. Conquests were conquests, and stupid men had to brag about them, often embellishing the facts. Tonight was no different. There was talk of the new assistant, and how she was "able" and "willing" to "assist" with many things was the claim from one of the group. Another asked for her number, quickly grabbing a pretend pen and paper in jest. Tonight he made a fatal mistake by opening his mouth.

He told the others he had found the ultimate stress reliever. A pipeline of beautiful women, minus the fuss and muss. Men had been willing to pay for sex through the ages. He slyly told him his secret, which was his car rental agency. He said it specialized in cars of the Asian make, fast and sleek, with low mileage. He went into great detail that night about his adventures and exploits, fueled by the alcohol, and it came pouring out. He was the big winner in their testosterone competition! But it was also his biggest mistake.

His name was Thad Sokol.

CHAPTER SIXTY-THREE

ONE TRUE LOVE

She had met him in the bar where all transactions started. He was quiet and alone, and she had to be the aggressor. She slowly worked her way up to him and asked if he would buy her a drink and they could get to know each other. He informed her that he did not drink, but he would gladly buy her one. They had a nice conversation, as much as it could be with the language barrier.

He spoke of where he was from, although she sensed he was lying. She spoke of her home there in San Jose, what it was like to grow up there, her family, the culture. She asked him why he didn't get out to see the sites of the city. He told her that he was here to relax. She accepted this. After she finished her drink, they went back to his room. He was a good lover, giving, and receiving pleasure. He only made love to her that weekend. He did not want any other women, although there were many to choose from. It was easy work for her, and he had no problem paying. He would gladly have paid twice as much for her time.

When his stay was over, and it was time to leave, he asked her if she would be willing to be his wife, to live and love together forever. The only thing he required was that she move back to America with him and give up being a lady in waiting. She said she would, but after he went back, she could never find the right time to come to the States and be with him. He held out hope and helped her unconditionally. He would always come through for whatever she needed because she was the one true love of his life, even though they would never be together again.

Her name was Angelica Jaramillo.

CHAPTER SIXTY-FOUR

THE DOUBLE PLAY

She opened the page where she accessed her account on LetsDoThis.com, logged in, and read through the request for what she was searching. The message from the suitor read, "I would love to get to know you. I am looking for a long-term relationship with weekly meet-ups. I will need to understand what type of arrangement you'd like, along with the financial compensation you are looking for, please."

Well, he was at least polite, she thought to herself. She pulled up his profile and although he was older, he wasn't a complete monster. Could she do this? She questioned it from the very moment she typed in her information to the website. *Would her boyfriend find out? Would her mother find out? Could she live with herself?* These questions would play out in her mind for the next twenty-four hours until she made up her mind that she did not want to remain poor.

She logged back into her account and answered his questions. She responded, "I am interested and would agree to your terms for $1,200 per month." She paused then took the leap and hit send. She felt exhilarated. She figured combining this stipend with the money she earned at the bakery would be sufficient. Add to that the fact that she lived at home with her mother, limiting her responsibility for bills, she would be doing pretty well. She would be able to get some of the things that she had been missing out on. That made her smile.

Later that day she retrieved another message from him that read: "Can we meet to discuss everything?"

She replied, "Sure."

They met two days later for coffee in an out-of-the-way diner that he knew no one he knew would go to. He gave her the first installment in the amount she had requested. He could afford it because he was single with only himself to fend for. This was the beginning—or was it the end?

Her name was Shelly Lynn. His name was Bobby Reynolds.

CHAPTER SIXTY-FIVE

Nice Guys Finish Last

He spent hours cleaning his apartment. He didn't know why but it was the only thing that he could do to please her. She had always complained about his tidiness. He wanted her to love him. He stacked the bags in the kitchen so they could be taken out.

His life had been shattered. Twenty-four hours ago his biggest worry was getting his homework assignment completed. His life was busy, but he had everything he wanted, a girlfriend and, hopefully, a future. That was all shattered now. Without his girlfriend he felt like he was on the edge of a cliff deciding to jump or stay.

The detective had left hours ago after questioning him. He knew he would be the center of the investigation. But at this point did it really matter? He couldn't sleep, eat, or function. His computer was on but only so he could feel a little less alone. He longed to hear her voice one more time. He sat at the table and just stared blankly at the screen. Then they started appearing.

Pictures started popping up on his screen. At first he didn't understand, but then it became crystal clear what they were. They were pictures of her. But she wasn't alone.

He couldn't believe his eyes. She was making love to another man! There were so many of them it was overwhelming. Picture after picture. Then there was video with graphic noises coming out of the two lovers. They continued until what he had left inside his soul was gone. Then they were disappearing before his eyes as if they were never there. Were they just a figment of his imagination? Was he in the middle of a nervous breakdown?

No, he decided, *they were real.*

The images were burned into his brain forever. His ideal was shattered. There was nothing left. First, he got up and walked to his desk where he took out a piece of paper and a pen. He was shaking uncontrollably, most likely in shock. But he completed his note to her and set the pen down. Then he got up, walked to the drawer and found what he was looking for. The choice was made for him. He walked across the living room to the bathroom. He started drawing a bath. The water was very warm and comfortable. He sat and waited until the water was at the correct height. He undressed and neatly folded his clothes, setting them on the back of the toilet. He still wanted to please her by being tidy.

He climbed into the tub and brought the object up to his face looking at it for a split second before executing the final act. He wondered why his path had been altered. Did he do something wrong? It ended quickly. He simply went to sleep.

His name was Gavin Dean.

CHAPTER SIXTY-SIX

ACTION REACTION

The first incident happened in November of 1982. Mark called his cousin over to tell him something that couldn't wait. Thirty-five minutes after they hung up, his cousin arrived, and Mark suggested they go out on the porch where they could talk in private.

Mark was acting very nervous, fidgeting. He was trying to find the right words. He knew he was going to cause his cousin great anguish and that was the very last thing he wanted to do since they had been good friends since they were young.

Mark said, "Cuz, you know I love you, man, and I would never want to hurt you, but I warned you about this girl. I told you to have fun, but don't get too attached."

His cousin replied, "What's that supposed to mean? She's not cheating on me, I treat her way too well," he retorted, not wanting to believe anything was going on.

"Cuz, it's been happening for two months now. I know this because one of the guys on Ringgold's football team was telling me about this crazy little girl from Donora that a friend of his was fucking; you know, guy-talk stuff. So I asked her name. It just so happens it's a girl named Terri from Donora."

The color left his cousin's face. *How was this possible?*

He was working so hard to keep this girl's family from starving. He often bought groceries, clothes, and other things for her and her mom. His brain started crawling and he felt sick to his stomach. He could feel bile rising in his esophagus. He stormed out of Mark's house and drove straight to confront Terri at her house. He was full of rage, but holding onto hope that this was all just a terrible mistake. He hoped there was another Terri from Donora.

To her credit, she was pretty matter-of-fact about her indiscretion. She didn't leave anything to the imagination when she spoke of it. She confirmed it was a football player. She showed him the letterman's jacket the boy had given her to signify their being together.

He asked, "What about me?"

She just shrugged as if he was nothing.

He felt like he was the scum that sat on top of the pond. He clinched his fists, turned around, and left without even a word. His world just crashed down. He spent the next two weeks in his room devastated, his parents trying to console him.

Two weeks later she called him, asking to get back together. She told him that he was the one that she wanted to be with. His self-esteem was so low that he agreed to get back together. Later she confided to him that the other suitor's manhood was too large for her, and it hurt her. That was the reason for discontinuing the relationship. She made this comment to hurt him, and succeeded. This remark would be etched in his brain forever and mentally played back often.

The final event started on a Thursday in early March when Terri disappeared mysteriously without a trace. She didn't come home from school on the bus like usual. He checked with her mother, but she didn't know where she was. He started to panic. Had something bad happened to her? He drove around all night looking for her in every place he could think of. He was frantic and his brain felt like a million small bolts of lightning were passing through it over and over again. Then, as if magically appearing out of thin air, she reappeared on Sunday night with not a care in the world as she strolled in the front door with a cocky look on her face. He asked where she had been.

She replied, "None of your fucking business!"

Later her mother had told him that she had been with some "nasty boy." That was the final straw. He confronted her, and once again, she had no problem telling him about the other person. He was fully enraged so he pinned her to the bed, his hand holding her arms above her head and his legs pinning her body down by putting his weight on her hips.

She looked up and said, "You want to hit me, just do it!" with venom in her voice.

He did want to hit her. He wanted her to feel the pain that he was feeling. His blood pressure was through the roof, his brain was itching like a million small bugs were crawling around inside his skull. But he stopped, got off, and shook his head back and forth, amazed at his own stupidity. He got up and walked out. But his moral code was destroyed forever, and his dark side was brought to life.

His name was…

Epilogue

May 15, 2043

The note read:

I have lived a good life. I have seen the world. I have lived and loved. I am now even with the world. I leave no debts unpaid, and I feel my work is done.

The note was handwritten. It was placed by a tree along with a small caliber handgun and silencer. The view overlooked a pond where the sun set daily. The house was set afire and by the time the fire department arrived and was able to fully extinguish it, there was not much left. They found the charred remains of an elderly man. There was no identification possible.

Rest in Peace, Unknown.

www.ingramcontent.com/pod-product-compliance
Lightning Source LLC
Chambersburg PA
CBHW061248210726
48293CB00003B/892